A Dangerous Yes

Unleashing a generation to say yes to the things of God

Michael Medori

A Dangerous Yes

Copyright © 2020 Michael Medori

All rights reserved.

Edited by: Sara Laurence

Cover Designed by: Ash Ahern International

Unless otherwise noted, scripture quotations are taken
from the Holy Bible, English Standard Version

ISBN: 978-0-578-66734-8

DEDICATION

To Becca…You make life worth living…

CONTENTS

THE MOST IMPORTANT DECISION OF YOUR LIFE

Saying yes is dangerous.

Let's just throw that out there early on. Saying yes to *another* thing in our already busy world is very dangerous and a bit unnerving.

To be honest, when I first felt that the Lord was calling me to say yes to everything He was leading me to, I thought the same. *"My schedule is already way too busy. I already have way too much going on. There's no more room to say yes to anything else."*

Saying yes to another thing just didn't even seem feasible.

Let's imagine our lives like a dinner plate. A thanksgiving plate to be exact.

I don't know about you, but my Thanksgiving plate weighs about as much as a newborn baby. Ham and Turkey set the foundation, while mashed potatoes, sweet potato soufflé, and cream corn are running down the side.

The only difference is, with our lives, the ham is more like soccer practices and the sweet potato soufflé is more like gymnastics and the corn is like the 50 million other things we're trying to be a part of.

I'm not sure if you've recognized this or not, but we are way too busy.

The natural tendency is to look at the plate and say, *"I'll take this off and this off, everything else stays."*

But what if there was a better way?

What if instead of taking one or two things off the plate, what if God was calling you to completely remove everything from your plate, reevaluate, so you could *only* put back the things He is calling you to say yes to?

God's desire, and I believe the heart of this book, is to lead you, like a 50,000-pound magnet, pulling you into the fullness of life and joy found by living in perfect rhythm with your Heavenly Father.

Saying yes is dangerous.

However, saying yes to the right thing, is a thrill.

The Most Important Decision of Your Life

I'm a pretty upbeat kind of guy. In fact, sometimes my optimism can be a little frustrating. I am totally, unapologetically *that* guy.

Friends have told me that my stamp of approval has completely lost its weight at this point. That's because I'm always the guy who says things like, *"This is the best burger I've ever eaten! That was the best show I've ever been to! That was such a great message!"*

You know, *that* guy.

I'm him.

I have become painfully aware of how my excitement levels are a bit weird. I love to encourage people, I put too many exclamation points in emails, I make everything out to be the "best", and I definitely overuse emoji's.

Sue my why don't you.

When I first met my wife, she told me it seemed like I had sun rays coming out of my butt. Yeah, she definitely saw me as *that* guy.

But today, I'm different. Today *feels* different. Today, my heart is being squeezed like a towel ringing out gallons of water.

That guy is nowhere in sight.

Almost 24 hours ago, our ministry team packed up three cars, hopped in, and drove 60 miles to the next town over. I was speaking to a group of young adults, and our teams were leading worship. We rented a cabin for the entire team, eager to see all that God was going to do. We came in expecting God to move in the lives of the people we would encounter that weekend and set their lives on a heavenly trajectory like a rocket shooting into the night sky.

We arrived a few hours before people started showing up. I walked into a back office so I could take some time to quiet myself, and to pray through my notes. I was speaking on the subject of saying yes to the things of God. Little did I know, that message was going to impact *me* more than anyone else in the room.

The lights dimmed, and the worship team was about to start. We could hardly wait any longer. Our team stood in the back room, hands clammy, hearts full, smiles from cheek to cheek. Jesus, the Almighty, was here, and we could sense it deep down to our cores.

Have you ever experienced anything like that? A moment you truly believed that a piece of heaven was coming down and touching Earth? We were in that moment.

About five minutes into this moment with God, with tears rolling down my face, I opened my eyes, fully believing that everyone else was experiencing the same thing I was. I opened my eyes believing that every heart in the building would be responding at the wonder of this incredible Jesus. I mean come on, how awesome is this? The Holy Spirit was so evident in the room!

But when I opened my eyes, what I found wasn't at all what I was expecting. *There was nothing.* Out of an entire auditorium of young adults, I could count on one hand the amount of people engaged in worship. There were a few yawns, a few looks down at cell phones, one guy was even checking his watch, but there was hardly any worship happening in the room.

My heart was totally crushed.

Now you have to understand, that isn't a normal experience for me. At the church my wife and I started just under two years ago, it's normal for people to openly respond in worship. It's normal for people to be down on their knees, hands lifted, pressing into the Lord. That's normal to us.

But what I realized that night is that what we experience at our home church every week is not necessarily 'normal' in the American Church culture we live in.

The scary part was that I knew these people. I knew they had the capacity to be engaged and excited about something. These same people would go crazy over a football game—a bunch of men running around in spandex chasing other men in spandex with a ball. Where was that kind of excitement? Where was *that* kind of passion?

As I was looking over a sea of students, everything became much clearer. My eyes shifted to the section of parents. These were the same moms and dads who most likely forced their kids to come that night. These were the same moms and dads hoping their kids would grow up and stay plugged into the church. These were the same moms and dads wanting their kids to say yes to the things of God. But unfortunately, these were also the same moms and dads who didn't even stand during worship, were pre-occupied by their phones and seemingly bored at the very presence of the One who gave it all for them. The same parents who wanted their kids to have an exciting relationship with God seemed unengaged in their own relationship with Him.

In that moment, I realized we had a major problem on our hands:

An entire generation of people has been lulled to sleep for the things of God, and they have passed down that baton of faith to the next generation who have become bored with the things of God. What we've produced is a generation who can get more excited about *Fortnite* than their Father. A generation who can get more excited about jerseys than Jesus. A generation who can be more excited about sports than their Savior. A generation who is saying an emphatic, "Yes!" just to the wrong things.

Your yes matters

If I can put this simply, your entire life is made up of lots and lots of things you've said yes to. Maybe we see our lives as this huge landscape of different experiences, places we've been, people we've met, jobs we've worked, and on and on and on. But I think when you break it all down, our entire lives are really just made up of all the different things we've said yes to along the way. And as a result, all the things we've said no to as well.

That's why your yes matters.

Your yes is more important than you think. What you say yes to matters because what you say yes to is ultimately shaping your entire destiny.

Fully come alive in Him

Saint Irenaeus once said, "Man fully alive *is* the glory of God."

Did you catch that? The glory of God *is* man fully alive. In other words, God is most glorified when men and women are fully alive in Him. Or maybe we could say it this way: We are most satisfied in Him when we say *yes* to the things that most glorify Him.

How tragic would it be if you spent your entire life never once seeing God move greatly on your behalf? This book is not to diagnose a problem, it's to offer a solution.

I want to lay before us a case. An opportunity for all of us to consider trading in our little stories, for the much bigger, much more important story of God that is happening all around us. Consider it an enhancement to your life—maybe even an upgrade—to die to ourselves so we can fully come alive in Him.

Somewhere along the way, we've gotten this flipped. We have traded the glorious gospel of Christ for our own Christian spin on the American Dream. We have become so enamored with the smaller stories of ourselves that we've missed the much more beautiful story of God happening all around us. We've negotiated our yes to the things that will make our stories as big as possible, but in doing so, we've missed out on saying yes to the massive, God-sized story happening all around us.

I hope that you will consider my context for just a moment. I didn't grow up in the church. I didn't come to know Jesus until I was 19 years old and didn't start truly following Him until I was 21. And now, some of the things that I have seen in the church truly confuse me. Think about it like this:

- How long would you continue going to Burger King if they didn't serve hamburgers?
- How long would you continue to go to a gas station if they didn't have any gas?
- How long would you sit in the local theatre with popcorn stained floors if the movie didn't play?
- How many times would you go back to a bowling alley if they didn't have any bowling balls available?

Do you see where I'm going with this?

How long will you and I continue to settle for anything less than the main point of life? Even harder than that, how long will we continue to live mundane spiritual lives when there is a God-sized destiny on the other side of your yes?

That's what this book is all about.

Storing up

John Piper put it this way in his book, *Desiring God*: "God is most glorified in me when I am most satisfied in Him."

Are you satisfied with your life? I'm not talking about the boat, or the house, or the things you've accumulated here on Earth. I'm talking about when it's your time to leave

Earth and enter into eternity with your Maker, are you satisfied with the treasures that you've stored up in heaven? If the answer is no, then saying *yes* is for you.

Let me say something to you that maybe nobody has ever said to you:

You are anointed.

You have been graced with gifts, talents, and skills. Gifts that weren't given to you by man, but by God. The good news of the gospel is that God wants you to be in relationship with Him, absolutely. But the part of the gospel that no one really talks about, is that He wants to use those gifts and talents that He's entrusted to you to make a real kingdom impact in the earth.

Have you ever stopped to consider that fact? That God actually has something more for you than just punching a clock from 9-5? Have you ever considered for a moment that Almighty God has more for you than just going from your dorm room to the classroom and back to the dorm room? Have you ever stopped to consider that God has more for your life than going home, putting your pajamas on, eating a bag of chips, and watching *The Office* for 3 hours? As amazing as that sounds, have you considered that God has bigger, more inspiring plans for what the purpose of your life could be?

What do you expect?

Before we go any further, let me do something that I love to do at our home church. When I'm about to share something that's a little bit hard or uncomfortable, I like to preface it with, "An elephant is about to walk in the room." Rather than everybody squirming and wondering if they should awkwardly laugh or not, sometimes it's so much easier to just call out the elephant in the room when he walks in.

So, a little heads up: The elephant is about to walk into this book.

Let me remind you of a quick story. You remember King David, right? He was the emotional man who wrote a majority of the book of Psalms. He had a few mess ups in his story, didn't he? But his *mess up* became a *set up* for God to *show up*.

In 1 Chronicles, we find out that David had shed so much blood in war, God told him he was not going to build the temple God promised the Israelites. So, David had two options: He could sulk in the corner, or he could do something with the promise God had spoken over his family.

Now this is where the story gets juicy! Because rather than sulking in the corner, David set up his son, Solomon, to be successful in the things of God and build the temple. He provided Solomon with all the wood, the exact measurements of the temple, and even went as far as providing the lamps and the weight in gold and silver. Literally everything Solomon needed to build the temple was provided to him by his father, David—the same guy who shed a massive amount of blood in war. What a great dad!

So, what's the takeaway here? Well, for starters, it's never too late to be used by God. Even after David royally screwed up, he still said yes to God using him. He still fulfilled his purpose.

But more importantly than that: When you give the next generation what they need to be successful, what can you expect? Hopefully success. When you plant seeds in the ground, at some point you can expect a harvest. Farmers don't hold a funeral service when they put seeds in the ground. They expectantly and joyfully wait on the seed to take root and begin to grow.

So, what happens when you pass down a faith that you yourself aren't very excited about? Do you expect to see a generation set ablaze for the things of God? Do you expect to see your children passionate about a relationship with Jesus? This is one of those times where we have to face the brutal facts and let the elephant walk in the room. Because the answer is unfortunately, *no*.

What we will undoubtedly see is an entire generation of people who care very little about the things of God. We will see an entire generation who are wishy washy in their faith. We will see an entire generation of people who never get connected to a body of believers and slowly drift into the kingdom of themselves rather than building the Kingdom of God. Being a part of the global church won't be personal anymore; it will just be a chore that they check off until they become old enough to make their own decisions, walk away from the things of God, and miss out on the very destiny and purpose God has over their lives.

Here's the principle: Parents that treat the things of God as *optional* shouldn't be at all surprised when their children treat Jesus as *unnecessary*.

The point of it all

When I looked around that auditorium, I realized that an entire generation of people have become bored with the most interesting man that has ever walked this Earth: Jesus. I'm not just talking about millennials. I'm not just talking about Baby Boomers and Generation Z, I'm talking about all of us. Across the board, we are being lulled to sleep in our relationship with God.

And by the way, the enemy loves it this way.

But I believe in the deepest part of my heart, things are about to change. A generation of people are rising up who will not settle for mediocre, but rather will be unleashed to say yes to the things of God in the earth.

As I sat in that auditorium, I couldn't help but wonder how this happened. Jesus says in Matthew 12, *"Out of the abundance of the heart, the mouth speaks"* (Matthew 12:34).

Is that what was in their heart? A total disconnect from Almighty God?

It was a humbling moment for me as a young man. It was a moment when I had to just drop to my knees and repent. Have we settled for far less? Have we traded in the great thing for something far inferior? I know we all know *how* to worship, but it just wasn't happening.

In that moment, I made a commitment to my God, my wife, and myself. I would dedicate the rest of my life to the pursuit of seeing the Church of Jesus Christ come alive again for the things that actually matter. For the things that are significant. For the things that are eternal. No more settling.

As dangerous as this may be, I will say yes to the things of God, and I hope you will too.

You too?

I wonder if you are at a place in your life where you aren't satisfied in your relationship with God. Maybe you find yourself in a place where you love God, but you know there is more of Him that you haven't experienced yet.

The reality is, we have been entertained for far too long. We don't need *entertainment* Christianity any longer. We need *encounter* Christianity. We need the glory of God to come down and rock every person in the building. We need the glory that bears so much power, that the mere mention of the name of King Jesus, empowered by the Holy Spirit, causes sickness to fall back, cancer to bow down, and shame to flee. The glory that overcomes darkness by the light. The glory that causes depression and anxiety to fall back. The glory that leads people to be saved, repent of their old ways and step into the new. The glory that allows you to tangibly see God making a way in the wilderness and streams in the desert.

No more church as usual. No more simply *going* to church. But rather, we are stepping into *being* the church.

13

We must say *yes*.

I don't know about you, but that's what I want to be about. I don't care about lights, smoke, and being entertained; I want to have an encounter with God.

In a world where there's more noise, opinions, and experts than ever before, we need to hear from the Holy Spirit. We've become a generation who has become overloaded with *information,* but we are starving for *application* and *meditation.* Let me be the first to say if it hasn't been said already, we consume more content than our soul knows how to handle. We're about 3000 bible verses overweight because we never actually work them out.

It is true that while we are consuming more content than ever, we simultaneously are applying less than ever. We are quick to jump from podcast to podcast, sermon to sermon, and song to song without ever reflecting on the words and the content we just took into our hearts.

On this subject, J. I. Packer said in *Knowing God,* "It certainly makes it possible to learn a great deal secondhand about the practice of Christianity."

It's possible to know a lot about God simply from listening and learning from another person. There is nothing wrong with this, but when we recognize that we have the greatest teacher of all living within us, this is when the Church will see her brightest days.

If not you, then who?

Romans 10:14-15 says, *"How then will they call on him in whom they have not believed? And how are they to believe in Him of whom they have not heard? And how are they to hear without someone preaching? And how are they to preach unless they are sent? As it is written, 'How beautiful are the feet of those who preach the good news!'"*

In other words, how will they *know* unless we *go*? How can they believe unless someone points them to the One to believe in? This isn't about mustering something up on the inside of yourself, this is about a generation of people stepping into the things of God. This isn't a cry for people to muster up something on the inside of themselves to find more of a passion for God.

This is something totally different.

This is about awakening to the glory of God that is moving all around us. This is about Jesus being exalted to the highest place. It's more than a goose bump, and it's definitely more than a feeling. This is the Holy Spirit coming down in fire and making Himself real to His people. It's the family of God, in the house of God, experiencing the glory of God, and by the power of God, going out into the world as the light of God.

There are far too many people in our world who are hurting. There are far too many people in our world who are dying on the inside of themselves, who are suffering from anxiety and depression. There are far too many people considering suicide and battling cancer.

We need an encounter like no other. We do not need Church as usual, or Church as an organization. We need an encounter where something on the inside of us begins to awaken. We need an encounter where our hearts start racing, our palms become sweaty, and our boldness begins to rise up.

What happens when you say yes to God?

I'll tell you.

An entire generation of people are unleashed, unchained, unrestrained, and the landscape of the entire world begins to change. At some point we must make the decision that we are not going to settle for church as usual, but that we will step into everything God has for us.

You're closer than you think

Doesn't that sound incredible? When was the last time you woke up *excited* that it was Sunday morning? When was the last time you rushed through the front doors to get to the front row of the auditorium *expecting* to meet with Jesus? When was the last time you walked into your workplace or college campus with an anointing knowing that you are here on purpose and for a purpose? When was the last time you had the incredible privilege of being used by God in your sphere of influence?

That reality is closer than you think.

What you say yes to matters. What job you say yes to matters. What spouse you say yes to matters. What house you say yes to matters. And I'd like for you to consider, for just a moment, that there is something far more important that you say yes to. It's the most important decision of your life. In the balance of this decision stands freedom or bondage. In the balance of this decision stands a life of purpose or a life that's become stale.

This is the most important decision of your entire existence on this planet.

Experiencing the "abundant" life Jesus talks about is closer than you think. You are 1 word, 3 letters, 1 syllable away from it. You guessed it.

Yes.

Say yes to the things of God, step in fully with your whole heart, and we will begin to see an entire generation unleashed for the things of God. This is not a *moment* in history; this is a *movement* of history.

Saying yes is dangerous.

Will you join the Yes Generation?

THE MISSING KEY

We had *everything.*

We had our licenses and passports as back-up identification. We had all our bags and luggage. We had the noise cancelling headphones, gum, water, candy, and books to read. We were ready.

We had *everything.*

But I'll never forget that feeling as the wheels of a 757 Delta Jet screeched onto the runway at 184 mph in Atlanta, Georgia. I looked at my wife as we landed and asked her, *"Baby, do you have the keys to the car?"*

When I saw her face, I immediately knew the answer.

No.

We'd left our keys hanging on a key ring in my parents' home in Newark, Delaware. The sheer panic on Becca's face is humorous now, years later, but in the moment, it was not funny at all. We still debate to this day who left the keys behind. Becca is convinced it was me. Over the last few years, I've left my keys in more places than I can count and am notorious for losing them, so she has a strong argument against me.

Though we thought we had everything that day, we didn't. And the thing we'd forgotten was something incredibly important—something that would get us from point A to point B. The only thing that could get us to where we wanted to go was hanging on a key ring over 800 miles away.

For many of us, we have *everything*. We know our Bibles, we show up to church, and we have the resources to grow our faith more than ever. We have everything we need to do everything that God has called us to do.

In fact, scripture is clear on this in 2 Peter 1:3. It reads, *"For His divine power has bestowed on us [absolutely] everything necessary for a dynamic spiritual life and godliness, through true and personal knowledge of Him who called us by His own glory and excellence."*

Only along the way, we've forgotten the most important thing—the most important person. We have forgotten our spiritual keys—what will get us from point A to point B in this journey of saying yes.

We'll talk more about this in just a few pages.

Expectations and Experiences

For many of us, there is a gap between what we

expect and what we *experience.*

When I stepped off the plane in Atlanta, I was expecting to walk to my car, get in, and begin the two-hour journey home through the Appalachian Mountains, curving our way through the backroads of Georgia. Instead, we experienced something totally different.

Our lives are full of expectations and experiences, and I've learned to try and manage both for myself and for others.

Expectations are everywhere. In your job, your marriage, in relationships, in school, and even in church, there are expectations.

Author Brene Brown wrote a book called *Rising Strong.* In this book, she talks about something she calls "stealth expectations." She describes "stealth expectations" as the expectations we don't even know we have until they're not met. Oftentimes we get into situations where we find ourselves angry or frustrated and we wonder how we got there. According to Brown, it's most likely because we had an expectation that didn't get met.

If you find yourself in a moment of frustration saying, *"I just thought we would have _____,"* or, *"I just had my heart set on _____,"* that's a stealth expectation. Whether we realize it or not, we carry these expectations into everything that we do. Of course, having certain expectations isn't necessarily a bad thing. But here's the issue I've encountered when it comes to expectations: **The gap between your expectation and your experience is often the source of frustration.**

Frustration lives in the gap between expectations and experiences. The bigger the gap between what you expect and what you experience, the bigger the frustration. The smaller the gap, the smaller the frustration.

Here's my point: Even your faith has an expectation. However, your faith is not based off of emotions or feelings alone; it's based in the Word of God. I love this reality because the Word gives me clear expectations when it comes to my faith. I can expect that as a carrier of the Holy Spirit inside of me, I can walk into a dark situation and light it up with the glory and love of God. I *can* be the light of the world and the salt of the Earth, like Jesus calls me to be. I *can* be a city on a hill that cannot and will not be hidden or shaken. That's a faith expectation rooted in Truth.

If my experience is different than my expectation in my faith, the Word reminds me that God is still in control. My faith gives me an expectation that because my God is eternal, He knows the beginning from the end. He is the Alpha and the Omega, the First and the Last, the Great I Am.

Sometimes I see God as a movie director. *(I know, my brain works in weird ways!)* Since He has already shot the opening and closing scenes, I can trust Him with all the scenes in the middle, too. He knows the whole story.

That's a faith expectation.

Don't miss this: What we're talking about is a faith expectation; not a hopeful wish. This is God's perfect and

Holy Word. So, we can be confident *"that He who began a good work in us will be faithful to bring it to completion on the day of Christ"* (Philippians 1:6).

But what happens when our experiences don't line up with our expectations when it comes to faith? Well quite frankly, when I look over the landscape of the American church, this is exactly what's happening. So many times we thought we would have been used by God in some big and amazing way, but now, maybe you're older, looking back on a life that didn't meet that expectation. We've got *everything*— the house, the cars, the nice kitchen countertops with the backsplash and all—but we're left unsatisfied and disappointed. Why? Because our faith experience has led to very little stock in Kingdom economics.

And this makes me wonder: How did we get here? When I look at the early church in the book of Acts, they had a *high* expectation. Like really high. Way high. So high that most people in our culture today would think some of the things they were praying and believing for were absolutely nuts. Yet to them, this was *normal.*

How about when Peter and John approached the lame beggar in Acts chapter 3? The beggar expected something from Peter and John, but guess what? Peter and John had an expectation, too. The beggar was hoping for a temporary fix, some money, but Peter and John were expecting eternal stock. Peter walked up to the beggar and said, *"Silver and Gold I do not have, but what I do have I give you. In the name of Jesus Christ of Nazareth, walk"* (Acts 3:6).

Now, let me say something important. When Peter and

John said "walk," they weren't taking a shot in the dark. It wasn't a hail Mary. It wasn't a, *Let's just see if this works,* kind of a thing. There was a confidence about them. There was an expectation that as soon as they declared *"in the name of Jesus Christ, walk"* that this man was going to get up and begin walking. That is insane! If you think the Bible is boring, trust me when I tell you that it's not. This is Hollywood type stuff right here!

Peter and John had an expectation that lined up with their experience. That dude stood up and began dancing and jumping through the temple. He was moving around so much that the people who recognized this man as the beggar *"were all filled with wonder and amazement at what had happened"* (Acts 3:10).

And this story is just one example! Time and time again through the book of Acts, we see followers of Christ have an experience that met their expectation.

Now if we can be honest, for many of us, our faith expectations and life experiences haven't lined up as often, have they? In fact, for many of us, our lives can be summed up like this: We had an expectation that didn't get met, and we were left feeling frustrated and exhausted with the process. The gap between our experience in life and our expectation from the Scripture has created spiritual frustration. And for many of us, the response is bitterness or fruitlessness in our faith. Maybe even for some, you have completely walked away from the faith as a result. *"I tried Christianity; it just didn't work."*

Why is Christianity of today so much different than the

Christianity of the early church? We're serving the same God. We're building the same church. Why is it so different for believers today?

I believe our answer lies in a person. The gap between your expectation and your experience is filled by a person. He's a person who is often neglected. He's a person who is often ignored, and certainly in the church, He is a person that we don't talk about enough. He is a part of the Godhead, yet He is often the forgotten piece of the puzzle.

I'm talking about the person of Holy Spirit.

This is awkward.

See, the story we looked at in Acts with the lame beggar really started in the chapter before on the day of Pentecost. Scripture says:

"All of them were filled with the Holy Spirit and began to speak in other tongues as the Spirit enabled them" (Acts 2:4).

I have found that verse to be one of the most controversial verses in all of Scripture. Are the gifts given in the first century still for today? Is speaking in tongues still for us today? Is the power of the Holy Spirit still needed for today?

I don't want to assume I know all the answers, but what I do know is this: from that day forward, *the change was undeniable.* The same Peter who was afraid and fearful for his life, was now preaching the gospel and thousands were being saved. The same John that fell asleep on Jesus was now fully alive. The same disciples who were constantly doubting, are now launching the church forward into every part of Europe, ultimately leading to where it is today. What started on the day of Pentecost continued with the lame beggar. And the story continued throughout the entire book of Acts.

What I believe the church of today is missing that the church of the 1st century had was a deep dependence on the Holy Spirit. Now before we go on, let me stop here and clarify some terms. I'm talking about the corporate Church, yes, but I'm also talking about the individual people of God—the people who want to say yes. In the 1st century, we had the power of God accomplishing the work of God in the people of God. And today, we've got natural, normal people trying to accomplish the supernatural work of God, *without the power of God.*

As a result, more people are getting hurt, and more people are leaving the church. More people are bored with their faith, and more people are saying the church isn't needed today. I believe all of this stems back to the same problem: **We're trying to do the *work* of God without the *power* of God. Our expectation is not meeting our experience, and we're left feeling spiritually frustrated.**

The same person, the Holy Spirit, that the early church depended on, and yearned for, and so desperately needed, is the same person who has almost been completely forgotten about in the church of today. In fact, for any church leaders reading this chapter, think back on the last seven days of your ministry. How much of it did you do without yearning for the supernatural power that comes only from Holy Spirit? I'm not just talking about praying five minutes before you go up to speak. I'm talking about the whole process. I'm talking about a yearning for the Holy Spirit to move in power. To use you in ways that you didn't even know were possible.

Could you imagine if we walked into the grocery store like this? Could you imagine if we raised our kids like this?

The possibility is endless.

The power to accomplish the purpose God has set out for you comes by the indwelling of the Holy Spirit. If we want to say yes, we *must* say yes to the person of Holy Spirit.

He is the One who leads us and lives inside of us. He is a person of the Godhead whom Scripture says empowers and teaches us. In John chapter 14, Jesus says this:

"But the Counselor, the Holy Spirit, whom the Father will send in my name, he will teach you all things, and bring to your remembrance all that I have said to you" (John 14:26).

In Ephesians chapter 4, Paul specifically writes to *Christians* to tell them:

"Do not grieve the Holy Spirit of God, by whom you were sealed for the day of redemption" (Ephesians 4:30).

Have we grieved the Holy Spirit of God by living a life seemingly without Him? By living a life that is not desperate and dependent on Him? I know I did for the longest time.

I think it's time to invite the Holy Spirit back into our lives. To invite Him back into the work God is calling us to. Without the power of God accomplishing the work of God, we can do nothing. We will only exhaust ourselves on the religious treadmill. But when we allow the Holy Spirit to work in us, we can see our faith expectations met with supernatural faith experiences.

Just lower the hoop

I was playing basketball one day with a bunch of younger kids. Apparently, they lower the hoop until you reach a certain age. When the hoop is lowered, I can do what I've always wanted to do since I was in 4th grade. As a 5-foot 8 short guy, I can get a running start, and with everything in me jump as high as I can and dunk the basketball. I know I probably shouldn't do this, but I would totally slam dunk on an 8-year-old. I am totally unashamed.

What I'm trying to say is when you lower the hoop, anybody can dunk.

The same concept is the major difference between the nominal Christian and the people who are willing to step into a dangerous yes towards the things of God. Someone who doesn't understand the authority and power inside of us as a Jesus follower would say, *"Just lower the hoop."*

In other words, just lower the expectation.

Because if you lower the expectation, then you can meet

and exceed it. You'll find happiness rather than disappointment.

But that's not how the Yes Generation should respond. The expectation does not lower; the expectation remains the same and we can trust it because it's rooted in God's Word.

I believe the church is on the verge of the greatest revival this world has ever seen. But in order to do it, we've got to step into the power of God to accomplish the work of God. Jesus says in John 8:

"If you abide in my word, you are truly my disciples, and you will know the truth, and the truth will set you free" (John 8:31-32).

If you *abide*. That word in the Greek language is "meno." It means "to remain, dwell, and to be kept continually in." In the second part of the verse, the word "know" comes from the word "ginosko." In the original language, that means "to intimately know." In fact, it was a Jewish idiom that was meant to talk about how a man *knows* his wife. You catching my drift? So, with those things in mind, you could read John 8 to say: "When you remain in the Word, you will intimately know the Truth."

But here's my point: How can you remain in the Word if you don't intimately know the One who reveals the Word?

Paul writes in 1 Corinthians 2:10: *"These things God has revealed to us through the Spirit. For the Spirit searches everything, even the depths of God."*

He goes on to say:

"Now we have received not the spirit of the world, but the Spirit who is from God, that we might understand the things freely given to us by God. And we impart this in words not taught by human wisdom but taught by the Spirit, interpreting spiritual truths to those who are spiritual" (1 Corinthians 2:12-13).

Did you catch the end? God has spiritual truths that He wants to reveal to spiritual people. Such truths that talk about the depths of God! Isn't that incredible? And the best part is, He wants to give them to us so that we might *freely* understand these things! God wants to reveal intimate truths by the Holy Spirit to those who are spiritual.

But do you know how Paul addresses the Corinthian church starting in chapter 3?

"But I, brothers, could not address you as spiritual people, but as people of the flesh, as infants in Christ" (1 Corinthians 3:1).

These people at the Corinthian church were Christians! Baby Christians, but Christians none the less. Paul wanted to reveal truths to them, but he felt like he couldn't. Why?

Because they didn't read the Word? No.

Because they didn't show up to church? Nope.

Because they didn't give in the offering plate? Negative.

Paul couldn't share truths with them because they were still infants in Christ. Is it possible that God wants to show you intimate truths through His Word but is unable to because you're unaware of the One who intimately reveals the deeper truths? That person is the Holy Spirit. God wants you to experience Him at a more intimate level, but it takes an awareness of the third person of the Godhead—the Holy Spirit—for the truths of His word to be revealed. There's a major difference between communicated knowledge and revealed knowledge.

Communicated knowledge is when you hear something, and even though it's true, you kind of forget about it over time.

Revealed knowledge is when you hear something that is true, and it ignites something in your life that you will never forget.

Have you ever been reminded of something your Pastor said over a year ago? Maybe even 5 years ago? That's revealed knowledge.

Only the Holy Spirit can reveal knowledge to your heart about the deeper things of God.

I believe deep down to my core that God has something so beautiful for your life. Something majestic. Something that will echo in eternity. I believe God is calling you to say yes. The first step is for you to remember the missing key. The first step is to begin intimately understanding the third person of the Godhead—the person of Holy Spirit.

After you read this chapter, I want to ask you to put this book down. I want you to stop and pray. Reflect. Be still for a few moments.

I want you to ask God to reveal the person of the Holy Spirit to you. I want you to pray for God the Father to make you more aware of the Holy Spirit in your life. Ask Him to fill you into all fullness of the Spirit. This is different than your salvation experience. This is being filled by the Spirit of God. It happened in Acts *all the time*. It's not as weird as many people have made it out to be. In fact, Jesus told the disciples right before the Day of Pentecost that there is one thing that is absolutely crucial you experience before you are sent out. They needed to be baptized in the Holy Spirit.

Acts 1:4-5:

"And while staying with them he charged them not to depart from Jerusalem, but to wait for the promise of the Father, which, he said, 'you heard from me, for John baptized with water, but before many days you shall be baptized with the Holy Spirit."

It took place in Acts 19:2 as well. *"And he said to them, did you receive the Holy Spirit when you believed? And they said, "No, we have not even heard that there is a Holy Spirit"* (Acts 19:2).

The believers didn't know anything about the Holy Spirit, much like believers of today.

Multiple times in 1 Corinthians chapters 12 through 14 we see the same thing unfolding.

John the Baptist said in Luke 3:16:

"I baptize you with water; but he who is mightier than I is coming, the thong of whose sandals I am not worthy to

untie; he will baptize you with the Holy Spirit and with fire."

Whew! Give me some of that!

Joel prophesied about this in Joel 2:28;

"And it shall come to pass afterward that I will pour out my Spirit on all flesh."

Peter quoted Joel just after the Holy Spirit fell on the day of Pentecost and thousands were saved.

The essence of being baptized in the Spirit is not weird, it's necessary. This is being empowered to know the deeper truths of God and being launched out into the world to do the *work* of God by the *power* of God.

Jesus said in John 16:7;

"It is to your advantage that I go away, for if I do not go away, the Helper will not come to you. But if I go, I will send him to you."

Paul said in Ephesians 5:18,

"Do not get drunk with wine, for that is debauchery, but rather, be filled with the Spirit."

That phrase "be filled" is the word "plerousthe," which actually would be better translated, *"be being filled."* This means to allow yourself to continually be made full. At some point, the oil in a lamp will go out. In the same way, the gas in your car will eventually run out. And unless you continually fill it back up, you won't get very far.

The same is true with your yes. If you don't keep filling yourself up with the truth of God, empowered by the Spirit, you won't go very far. I have found this to be the story of many Jesus followers. Maybe years ago, you said yes to God, but you've been working out of a faith in your own strength. Now, you're tired. You're worn out physically, spiritually, and mentally. Let me encourage you to step into the power source. Let your yes be sustained by the power source of the Holy Spirit. After all, you were never designed to carry this weight on your own.

I want so badly for you to say yes to everything God has on your life. But it's impossible to sustain it in your own strength. Lean into God. Lean into the Holy Spirit today. Be filled again with the passion and truths of God's Word over your life. I promise you, there will come a day when you will be so full of God that it will brim over into your life in such a beautiful, supernatural way.

You have everything you need to say yes and to begin this journey.

Just don't forget the most important thing. Don't forget the keys.

THIS IS AWKWARD

Sin.

Just the mention of that word might have you thinking, *Oh gosh, we're going to talk about that? Maybe I'll just skip to the next chapter...*

Here comes that elephant again...but here goes nothing. Talking about sin feels like the first time I ever watched Michael Scott in *The Office*. It's always a bit cringe-worthy, but let's give this a go...

Sin has basically become a cuss word in our culture. It's not a term we use openly, but it can be like kryptonite to the Yes Generation. Sin is to Christians what the green crystalline radiation was to Superman. I believe it is the number one destroyer of destiny. It will annihilate an anointing and it will choke out your calling.

That's why, even if it's uncomfortable, we have to talk about sin.

It would be challenging to talk about what it means to make a kingdom impact without talking about sin. Honestly, I wasn't super excited to talk about this subject. I just don't get pumped up to talk about sin. But I want you to know that I am writing this chapter because it's important. I'm writing it for your joy and ultimately, for God's glory. My intention is to *build* you up, never *beat* you up. Nobody needs *another* message that you walk away feeling completely beat up. My intention is to hopefully draw from Scripture to see how detrimental sin can be to the Yes Generation. My hope is to help you overcome it so that you can step *fully* into the life God has for you.

Part of making a dangerous yes, means cutting away all pre-meditated, calculated, and consistent sin in our lives. Of course, we're all going to stumble and fall. None of us are perfect! But what I am getting at is that we all have a crutch. We all have a struggle. We all have those sins we seem to keep returning to over and over and over again in our lives. Maybe it's porn. Maybe it's pride. Maybe it's a poor attitude. Maybe it's worry and you have worried yourself to death.

Whatever your crutch is, you have to fully release it in order to fully come alive as a part of the Yes Generation. You can't expect God's best when sin is involved, and I don't know about you, but I want God's best. I want everything He has for me. I want to experience God's best so much that even if it means He has to cut away some things in my life, I want Him to do it. I know that is a scary proposition, but I am that committed to seeing everything that God has promised over my life come to pass. I hope you are, too.

But the only way to have a resurrection is to have a death. The only way to have the resurrected power of Christ flowing in and through us is to put to death the earthly sin that is in us (Colossians 3:5).

Almost

A day is coming in all of our lives where our final chapter will end, and our book will be finished. In that moment, if you've given your life to Jesus and believed in Him, you will stand before the Lord, completely Holy and blameless in His sight. What a great day that will be!

I don't know about you, but as I'm lying on my deathbed, I have a hope for my final chapter. I hope that I can look back over my life and see all the things God has done.

All the victories, all the defeats.

All the mourning, all the dancing.

All the joys, all the sorrows.

I want to see it all.

When the movie of my life is showing on the screen, I hope that I can look back on my days and say with full confidence that I was more than just an "almost Christian." I want to be able to say with confidence that I was a full on, Bible-believing, God-fearing, Holy Spirit-filled, Jesus-following, soul-winning, devil-stomping, eternity-shaking Christian. And I really believe you're reading this book because you want the same for your own life.

But here's the truth: If we're going to reach that goal—if we're going to say yes to all that God has for us—then we've got to say no to sin *at all costs*.

At times, I can be pretty straight forward and blunt. I've noticed that people either really appreciate this or get easily offended by it. Of course, I don't mean anything negative by it; I just don't like to beat around the bush. When it comes to following Jesus, I tend to see it pretty straightforward: We either follow Him, or we don't. We either believe that He came to this planet, lived a perfect life, died a sinner's death, rose up from the grave, ascended into heaven, empowered us with the Holy Spirit, now seated at the right hand of the Father... Or we don't. There is no in between. There is no "almost" when it comes to Christianity. We either believe, or we don't.

The same is true when it comes to sin. There is no middle of the road here either. And to be honest, I think that's good news! I have a very addictive personality, so the last thing I need is someone telling me that it's okay to settle in sin. If I give myself permission to go there, then there's no going back.

Maybe you're like me, too. You don't need another person reminding you how much God loves you in your sin. You don't need another hype message disregarding the danger and impact of sin in your life.

Instead, what you and I need is someone to tell us with 100% grace and 100% truth to cut the sin out of our lives completely. Sin is like acid on the skin that needs to be removed with a scalpel. It is like fire that needs to be fully extinguished. It's like a tumor that needs to be removed. But for a tumor to be removed, it takes surgery. It takes a cutting away. It's not joyful, and it's certainly not fun. But it is crucial for the Yes Generation. Sin is the stumbling block to seeing God's plans and purposes fulfilled in our lives. And if we let it remain unchecked, it will be the ultimate destroyer to the destiny God has dreamed for our lives.

Misdiagnosed

Imagine you're taking your grandmother or someone you love to the doctor's office. You're worried about getting the results back from her cancer report. Your palms are sweaty. Your stomach is tied in knots like a Philly pretzel. You're anxious yet hopeful—somehow full of faith and worried all at the same time.

Now, imagine a group of doctors huddled together in a back office. The room is quiet and the off-white, stale walls add to this dreary situation. They are all looking at your grandmother's report and every one of the doctors make the clear, obvious decision: *It's cancer.*

Somehow, the room becomes even more bland. The sterile room has absolutely no life to it and any bit of hope in the room has been sucked out like a vacuum. There's no way around it. As terrible as it is, the results are clear: *Your grandmother is officially a cancer patient.*

The doctors begin talking. "How in the world are we going

to break the news to her? I mean, this is hard stuff here. It's uncomfortable!"

One doctor in particular speaks up. "I'm worried I will offend her if I tell her she has cancer. The good news is, we have the very thing that will remove the disease from her body, but this is going to upset her deeply when we tell her the news."

The doctors go back and forth trying to figure out a way to break the news. An argument breaks out in the room as they try to figure out how to proceed. Finally, after a long discussion, the doctors come to a conclusion.

Rather than offending or upsetting the patient, they decide to tell your grandmother that she only has a cold. The doctors agree, "We'll send her off with Benadryl and be done with it."

Shew! Conflict avoided...

Crazy, right? Tell me you wouldn't put those doctors in jail for malpractice! They knew what the disease was, and they even had the cure! Yet they were so worried about offending or upsetting your grandmother that they would rather misdiagnose her. They'd rather give her a "cure" that they know is going to kill her than risk having a hard conversation. Anyone with a brain knows that's crazy. *That's not good medicine!*

Now, let's put it back into the context of our faith. The disease of sin is going to kill us. But if we know Jesus, then we know there is a cure. Yet so often we're afraid of upsetting or offending so we opt not to talk about it at all.

We misdiagnose things in our lives, calling them "issues," or "struggles, or "hardships." And while that misdiagnosis might work for us for a moment, it will ultimately destroy us. Why? Because we aren't treating the real problem; we aren't diagnosing it as sin.

I know sin isn't super sexy, and it's definitely not popular to talk about. (I kind of feel like Ricky Bobby in *Talladega Nights* when he doesn't know what to do with his hands.) But just because something is *unpopular* doesn't mean it's not *true*. Even if it's hard to come to grips with, it would be so much better to call it like it is than to treat it like it's something that it's not.

Something I have noticed in my own life is that *sin always has death on its mind.* That's scary! The milder you make the label, the more potent you make the poison. Treating sin like it's not that big of a deal is dangerous. It's literally killing an entire generation.

But the good news is that there is a cure for the disease of sin! There's a cure for the weariness in our hearts. There's a cure for the weight that feels so heavy. It's the blood of Jesus, shed for every sin that has ever and will ever be committed! It's only by the blood of Jesus that we can be truly set free from our sin.

The blood of Jesus covers our sin unto salvation, and the Holy Spirit empowers us for sanctification to walk in holiness and godliness.

But in order to call on that power, we have to first recognize our need for it. And the lack of conviction to call sin what it is makes it difficult for us to see our need for a cure.

I have a feeling I know what some are thinking right now. *Those Millennials. You're so right Mike, sin is killing your generation. Lord you need to do something about those Millennials.*

Let's stop right there, because the worst thing we can do right now is think of someone else. The worst thing we can do is put our minds on "that person" who needs to read this chapter. Instead, we need to keep our eyes on our own hearts. The best thing we can do is look introspectively and say, "God, is this one for me?"

It's so easy to look across generations, and think the problem is somebody else's. So, can I just suggest something here? Sin is a multi-generational issue. It's an issue that affects Baby Boomers as much as it does Generation X and Millennials. Sin does not discriminate, and it does not differentiate. Sin will come after anyone and everyone who opens the door to destroy and corrode the very soul that God has placed inside of you.

He said what?

But you don't just have to take my word for it. Jesus said this in Matthew 5:29: *"If your hand causes you to stumble then cut it off."*

If I was preaching this verse from the platform, I'd stop right here and say, "Turn to the person next to you and say,

'Ouch!'" That's a pretty intense statement! In fact, if Jesus was a pastor of an American church, this statement right here might cause a modern-day exodus from His church!

But stick with me because I don't want you to miss this. Jesus didn't hold back when it came to sin. And that's very much intentional. He gives a pretty radical picture of what we need to do to take care of it. If you've got something in your life that is so powerful ruling over you, then you've got to do the most extreme, forceful thing you can possibly do to get rid of it completely. You need to take serious action. You can't just sit back and go, *"Well I'm just really wrestling with this right now. I'm just working through some issues. Just give me some time, and I'll get around to it."* No, you need to face it head on. You need to take serious measures to make sure you get rid of whatever the enemy has backed up and parked in the driveway of your life to keep you from the very thing God has been dreaming about for your life.

If a doctor told you that you had a massive tumor growing in your body and recommended immediate surgery so that you could continue to live life, I don't think your response would be, *"I'll get around to it. Just give me some time. I really need to weigh the options."* Of course not! It's life or death! If you don't deal with it, you're going to die! The same is true with sin. It's corrupting your very soul. It's crushing your calling. It's destroying your destiny. And it's annihilating the anointing over your life.

In my own life, I think I've become a little too accommodating when it comes to sin. We wonder why we don't have any victory in our lives. We wonder why we're not walking and talking in the fullness of God. We're accommodating sin in our lives but wondering why our joy is fleeting. Even as I'm writing this chapter, God is touching on my heart, convicting and reminding me that I've got so much stuff in my own life that I'm accommodating.

Many of us know what the Bible says, but we still think, "I'll just keep this sin around a little longer." If that's where you are, then I believe this is a word from the throne room of heaven for you today:

You've got to move all that stuff out of your heart and stop allowing it to keep residency in your soul.

It's time to declare war on sin. It's time to take action on the sin in our lives. And the war starts now!

Don't be stupid

Sin makes us stupid.

I hope that doesn't offend you. I promise I'm a typically a really nice guy, but sin just really makes me really stupid.

Maybe you too?

Sin has a way of tricking us. It doesn't allow us to think logically. It plays reverse psychology on us. We know we shouldn't do the thing we know to be sin, and yet we think to ourselves, *this will be my last time.* And what happens? We find ourselves there again, don't we? Then, we promise that the next time will be the last time. And after that, the next time. *Tomorrow I'll quit, and eventually it'll all be over.* Our intentions are certainly good, but sin ultimately blinds us. It tricks us into believing we have it under control. It deceives us all the way to the grave.

Don't forget: ***Sin always has death on its mind.***

Nike did an ad campaign years ago with the tagline, "Yesterday, you said tomorrow." Their approach? If you're going to be a champion, a winner, or a victor, then you need to start *today*. You can't wait until tomorrow; you need to start *today*. Because if you wait until tomorrow, you will put it off until the next day, and the next day, and the next day, until suddenly you're ten years down the road and haven't gone anywhere different.

The Yes Generation is making the decision, we will start *today*. Yesterday, you said tomorrow. And tomorrow, you'll say tomorrow. Today is the best place to start. Today is a great day to confess before the Lord some of the deepest parts of your heart. He loves you way too much to leave you where you are.

To truly understand the heart of Jesus when it comes to sin, we have to fully come to the conclusion that sin is a *really* big deal. Sin has torn families apart. It's ripped marriages to shreds. It's corrupted the minds of men and women all over the world. That, my friends, is a *really* big deal.

If we're going to call ourselves Jesus followers, then we need to adopt His heart toward sin. And fortunately for us, Jesus makes His position on the subject overwhelmingly clear. He willingly went to the cross to be beaten beyond recognition and killed in order to defeat sin on our behalf. That, too, is a *really* big deal.

Since God is Just and Holy (meaning He is set apart), He always has to act within the consistency of His character. God cannot weaken sin, He can't wink at it, and He certainly can't pretend it's not there. He set the mark when it comes to sin, but it's a mark we have missed. In the economy of Christ, sin has to be dealt with. And dealt with is exactly what Jesus did. 2 Corinthians 5:21 says: *"For our sake he made him to be sin who knew no sin, so that in him we might become the righteousness of God."*

Don't miss this! It's *became* and *become*. Jesus became our sin, so we could become righteous. In other words, Jesus assumed your position in sin, so that you could assume His position in glory.

Paul said one time that God would pour out all of His wrath on all sin (Romans 1:18). Paul said in the same book of Romans that "the wages of sin is death" (Romans 6:23). I mean come on, death?! That's huge!

I think sometimes we read that verse to be more like, "The wages of sin is *hurt*. The wages of sin is *guilt*. The wages of sin is *shame."* Those things aren't good, but they feel a little softer, don't they? Death? Well, that's a bit extreme! But here's the reality: Sin really is that big of a deal! Every time you and I sin, death creeps into our lives.

Now you might say, "Well Mike, thankfully I'm saved. I've been bought by the blood, which means I'm on my way to heaven. It might not be a mansion on a hill, but it'll be a shack on the backside of glory. I'm good." And while it's true—if you've been saved you are going to heaven and God does have a mansion for you (just don't ever say it's a shack on the backside of glory because that's insulting to the architect)—you need to understand that there's more to it than that. It's possible to go to heaven while simultaneously dying in little areas of your life along the way. It's possible to be a Christian without dealing with the places where God wants to lift you higher—the places where you've let death creep in. Those places where God wanted to give you breakthrough, but porn crept in and stole it. Those places where God wanted to use you immeasurably, more abundantly than you could have ever imagined, yet pride crept in and stole it. It's possible to go to heaven while simultaneously having miniature funerals along the way.

That's not the version of Christianity I want you to say yes to, and that was certainly never God's design.

In 2 Corinthians 3:18, Paul says: *"With unveiled face, beholding the glory of the Lord, we are being transformed into the same image from one degree of glory to another."* God's design from the very beginning was that we would look like Jesus, the author and perfecter of our faith (Hebrews 12:2). That means we should be going from glory to glory and strength to strength, not glory to death and strength to weakness along the journey to heaven. But the only way to go from glory to glory is to declare war on sin.

I love the way Genesis 4:7 puts it: *"Sin is crouching at your door. It desires to have you, but you must rule over it."* Sin starts off small; it crouches down to make you think it's no big deal. And when sin is small, we must crush it. We must rule and reign over it. **Because if we don't become the victor over our sin, it won't take long before we will become the victim of our sin.**

Cut out the right things

Something that often marvels me about God is the way He uniquely designed every single one of us. We all have our quirks. We all have the things we're really great at and the things we're not so great at. We all have the things we're passionate about and the things we're not so passionate about. We're all uniquely designed by Him.

God has uniquely wired you *to be you*. As a part of the Yes Generation, we must remember that there are things God will call all of us to cut away in our lives. It's our job to make sure we are cutting away the right things.

But if we're not careful, this could quickly become a religious duty rather than a joyful delight. Let me give you an example. David is one of my favorite people to read about in history. His story is phenomenal. He was patient, yet strong. He was humble, yet honest. He worshipped, yet wept. One moment we see Him fending off lions and bears, and the next we find him crying out before the Lord. I think he is the ultimate Rambo. He would definitely be my first pick to play William Wallace in *Braveheart*.

One thing I love about David is that God described him as "a man after my own heart." I think one of the reasons God described him like this is because David was honest with where he was. He was quick to repent, and he was quick to give God praise. He didn't hold anything back. He spilled his whole heart out on the table for everyone to one day read. David was real about the condition of his heart.

During David's life, God called him to cut away a lot of himself. David's sanctification process is undoubtedly the most put on display throughout all of Scripture. And here's why I think that's so important for us: David cut away a lot of things in his life, but he never cut away who God made him to be.

David had a lustful eye for Bathsheba. He had a murderous heart towards Bathsheba's husband. There was a lot of cutting away that God did in David. But the key is this: He cut away the right things, never the wrong things. He cut away sin, while keeping his God-made wiring. David continued to write poetry. He continued to play the harp. He continued to dance before the Lord. David cut away the right things, while simultaneously staying true to who God made him to be.

Practical steps

I think all of us have lived long enough to say we've faced a really challenging season of life. If you haven't, just wait. In this life, challenge is inevitable. Jesus even said: *"In this world, you will have trouble. But take heart! I have overcome the world" (John 16:33).*

In those moments of trouble, who are you going to lean on? Let me guess. The Christian answer you're thinking is Jesus, of course.

But what does it really look like to lean on Jesus? Well, it looks like a lot of things, but can I give you just one super practical piece of advice in this area? You need three people in your life who you can also lean on to hold you accountable. They will remind you of who you are, they will remind you where to run, and they will let you know when you're slipping. I've got a group of men in my life who hold me accountable. They love me too much to see me slip into sin patterns. *They see the calling God has put in my life, and they know it's too valuable to let sin destroy it.*

Choose wisely. Think prayerfully about getting some friends around you who can keep you headed in the right direction. Let them in. Don't put up any walls. Let them see deep into your heart.

I promise, you'll never regret it.

Accountability is one of the most powerful, practical tools that God has given to us as His beloved children. It's one of the best things we can say yes to in the war against sin.

PANCAKES AND BACON

It felt like it had been a lifetime.

In reality, it had only been about six weeks, but when you're in a season like the one my wife and I were in at the time, it might as well have been forever.

It was a season of life where it felt like our lives were moving at a million miles per hour. No rest. No stopping. No sleeping. Because after all, who has time for that? There are things that need to get done. Places we need to go. People we need to see.

Have you ever been in a season like this? Maybe you're in one right now. Everything feels like it's coming at you like flaming arrows flying through the night sky. Your kids have places they need to be. Your boss is working your fingers to the bone. And your marriage is just not quite clicking on all cylinders. It's a never-ending, never-ceasing nightmare that you can't wait to get out of.

My wife, Becca, and I know this feeling all too well. It was just a few years ago when we were in this season, but we knew it was going to end soon with a glorious vacation we had scheduled in the hills of Alaska. We couldn't wait to get out of the everyday, whirlwind of our life—to disconnect, recharge, and really try to hear from God.

When we finally found ourselves walking through the foothills of Alaska, we were amazed. Looking up at the massive, towering cliffs that surrounded us, the jagged, Alaskan mountains appeared to have been personally filed into sharp rocks by God Himself. As we were walking on the dusty, wet hiking trails, we saw all kinds of animals— moose, birds, small animals, large animals. Every part of creation we could have ever imagined, we saw on this hike. It was breath taking.

The cool, light air going in and out of our lungs as we paced through the hills of Alaska while breaking a small sweat. The small, thin vests we put on during the cold morning had now come off as the temperature rose around us.

It was one of the most beautiful places we have ever been.

Then it happened.

Suddenly, Becca stopped and said a few of the most glorious words I'd heard in a long time.

"Mike, I think I just heard a word from the Lord."

Her words brought a freshness to my soul the moment they left her lips. In that moment, I couldn't believe it. I jumped out of my boots and proclaimed, *"I think I may have just heard from the Lord, too!"*

Now before you go thinking we're insane, I need you to know it wasn't a booming voice speaking out loud or anything like that. It was simply an impression that God made on our hearts as we were walking through His creation.

We decided that we were going to say the words we heard individually out loud in the same moment. But before I had a chance to speak, Becca, in all of her excitement, blurted out her word:

Simplify.

My jaw hit the floor.

My reply? *"That's exactly the word God spoke to me, too."*

I'd never experienced a moment like this. At the same time, in the same moment, God spoke the same word to us.

Simplify.

There was so much excitement and peace pulsing through our bloodstreams. We both knew what our next steps were to be when we got home.

Our life was too busy. We were living our lives at 100 mph with no indication of slowing down. Something needed to change.

Maybe you've been there, too?

Flip Phones

We made the choice that we were going to disconnect from the things the world says we should be connected to. We couldn't take it any longer. Too much social media, too many emails, too many texts and phone calls to respond to. Things were moving at a pace that was unsustainable for us. Something needed to change.

It's been a year since we heard that word, *simplify*. And in that year, we've made every effort to respond and follow God's leading by trying to do just that: simplify. There was a season where we went back to flip phones, yes flip phones. It was the most frustrating, beautiful, annoying, wonderful experience of my entire life. We deleted our social media platforms for a season, cancelled our television subscriptions, sold two businesses we owned, and put our house on the market in order to downsize. The list goes on and on, but it's been the craziest, most beautiful journey I've ever embarked on.

I tell you that story to say this: We were so busy in our everyday lives that we *could not hear from God.* But when we stepped back and made space to listen, we discovered He was speaking the whole time, we just couldn't hear Him in the midst of all the noise.

This is such a common occurrence in American Christianity. People want to say yes to the things of God in their lives, but have no idea what they're saying yes to. Why? Because they can't hear from God. And what good is it to say yes to God when you can't hear what He's asking you to say yes to?

Less talking, more listening

Have you ever met someone who seems to only listen so that they can eventually talk? It doesn't even really matter what you're saying to them, because they aren't listening, really. They're thinking about what they're going to say next. They just can't wait to tell you what's on their mind.

In reality, I think this is the approach we take with God sometimes. We say we're listening, but if we're honest, it's only because we want to speak.

We pray, *"God I want to hear from you! Please! Show me your ways! Show me your heart! Show me your desires for my life! Show me anything God!"* And then just as quickly as the words leave our lips, we say, "Amen." Then, we're gone. We get up, walk away, and move on to do whatever it is we have next on the list. We pray, but never stop speaking long enough to listen. We don't slow down long enough to hear what God really wants to say.

How can we expect to hear from God unless we slow down? How can we expect to hear from Him when there is *so much noise* in our world?

For my wife and I, it took going to another part of the world to get out of our normal rhythm of life in order to find the rhythm of God's rest and actually slow down long enough to hear His voice clearly. And when we did, He did not disappoint. When we did, we got the greatest revelation we've had in our entire marriage.

Simplify.

We had to slow down to hear it. And I think that's true for all of us!

If we are going to be a part of the Yes Generation, then we need to talk less and listen more. We need to stop with all the busy and start with the intentional. We need to make space and time to clearly hear God's voice asking us to say yes.

Silence and Solitude

If we want to hear from God, I think we need to find silence and solitude as much as we possibly can. Jesus did this often. He modeled this for us, but very few of His followers actually follow His example. Why is that?

I think it's because, in today's culture, we feel the need to prove just how busy we are.

When I talk to people, I like to ask them a weird question. Sometimes they've never been asked this question, and it stops them in their tracks. I think it makes them think.

The question is this: "How's your soul? How's the inside version of you doing?"

I'd be willing to bet if you listen closely, you'll begin to hear a common theme in the replies.

"Man, I'm busy."

"Things have been nuts!"

"Crazy busy! But busy is a good thing, right?"

Is it? Is being busy all the time the way God designed us to live our lives?

Let me give you some encouragement: there is not one time in scripture where God commands you to be busy.

But busy is certainly the way American culture wants us to live our lives! It's almost as if we'd feel inferior if we told people, "You know what? Actually, I'm not busy right now. It's a really great season for our family. We're spending a lot of time together at the house and there just isn't a whole lot going on."

Wait, what? You're not busy? Psst! How lazy!

Believe me, I get it! Pastors are the worst about this. And to be honest, there's a little part of me that feels guilty when I'm not busy.

Like should I be doing more?

Should I be involved in 1 million different things like everybody else?

I mean after all, I'm a Pastor. This is what we do!

I'll never forget when we started applying this simplify method to our lives. Within just a few weeks of cutting everything from our schedule, somebody came up and said, *"Mike, y'all must be so busy! Y'all do so much!"*

Rather than telling this guy the truth—that we were slowing down and trying to simplify—I blurted out, "Yes, we're crazy busy right now."

What?!

Why did I blatantly lie to him? I'll tell you: I was embarrassed of not being busy. I felt insecure.

And then I came across a verse of scripture that has wrecked my world. It's found in Hebrews chapter 13, verse 7.

"Remember your leaders, who spoke the word of God to you."

Uh-oh. That's me...

"Consider the outcome of their way of life and imitate their faith."

Wait. Imitate my faith?

See when we live lives that are similar to the way someone who doesn't follow Jesus lives, we don't give people permission to simplify and get back to the original life God designed for us in the Garden of Eden.

In our culture we've come to believe the lie that down time is wasted time. We think we need to be going all the time, never stopping, never ceasing, always being productive. Even though studies have proven that this is detrimental for our health in more ways than one, we keep moving forward in the same manner.

But in this kind of lifestyle, it is nearly impossible to hear from the Lord.

There, I said it.

So, why don't I just go ahead and say what everybody wants to say and set the record straight.

I don't want to be busy anymore.

I'm tired of trying to do 1 million things to the glory of God.

It's not God's best for my life, and it's not God's best for your life either.

I don't want to be busy; I want to be *full*.

What's the difference? Busy implies things are coming at me uncontrollably. Full implies that I'm picking and choosing what's important to me. In other words, I get to control how "busy" I am. Or maybe more accurately, I get to control how "full" I am.

Let me give you an example from my own life. I've started scheduling rest on my calendar. The biblical word for this is *Sabbath*. So, when I schedule rest on my calendar, I am choosing to Sabbath. I'm giving myself 24 glorious hours of nothing but rest. 24 glorious hours of only doing the things that rejuvenate and reenergize my soul. I'm making space for what fills me up.

You see, a life that is busy and chaotic is powerless. It's weary, and worn out, and ultimately aimless. And the yes that God has been dreaming over your life is too important to fall to the wayside because of exhaustion and burn out.

The Big Ten

That's why Sabbath has been such a huge thing for me.

Sabbath is a verb. It's something you *do*. In Genesis 2:2 it says,

"And on the seventh day God finished his work that he had done, and he rested on the seventh day from all his work that he had done."

That word *rested* is the Hebrew word, 'Sabat'. it literally means "to Sabbath." It's a verb that means to cease and to rest. So, in other words, God labored for six days, and rested for one.

What blows my mind is that God didn't need to rest for Himself. Scripture says in Psalm 121 that He never sleeps, and He never slumbers. 2 Chronicles says that He is constantly looking to show Himself strong. God doesn't need to sleep; He doesn't need to rest; He chooses to rest.

This blows my mind; in God's rest, He was actually creating. At that point in time, there was no such thing as "rest". It hadn't been created yet. So, with His decision to rest, God was actually creating rest for the rest of us to rest. Insane, right?!

In Exodus 20, Moses was meeting with God on Mount Sinai, the place where he would receive the Ten Commandments. Now, if you grew up in church, then you know you don't mess with the Ten Commandments! These are the Big Ten. These are the *big sins*.

These are the list of commandments God gave His people to follow. And honestly, they're all pretty easy to understand.

Do not commit murder. Agreed.

Do not commit adultery. Winner winner.

Do not use the name of the Lord in vain. Yup.

Remember the Sabbath, and keep it holy.

Wait, what?

You mean to tell me that not murdering someone and taking a day of rest are in the same category?! It's *that* big of a deal to God?

Yup.

You can look all through the pages of your Bible to see over and over again just how important the Sabbath was to God. In fact, in Numbers 15, there's a story of a man who was picking up sticks on the Sabbath. What happened? They put a guard on him. I mean, this guy was an incessant, stick-picker-upper, why wouldn't they put a guard on him to stop this behavior?!

I wish I could put an emoji in this book because I would put the 'laughing out loud emoji' right there. This can't be serious! All he did was pick up sticks on the Sabbath and they put a guard on him?!

If that isn't weird enough, the story takes a turn for the

worse when God appoints that this man should be stoned to death. I mean, come on! This is insane! I've done much worse on my Sabbath I can promise you!

Stories likes these make me push away from my Bible to try and see the bigger picture.

But here's a principle I think we can learn from this man in Numbers 15: The Sabbath is incredibly important to God. And it's incredibly important to God because *you're important to God.*

Your health and well-being are important to God.

Your emotional stability is important to God.

Your spiritual balance is important to God.

Catch this; your family time is important to God. After all, He was the one who created family in the first place.

Hear me on this; your fishing time is important to God.

Let me free you with this thought: Your vacation time is important to God.

The reason the Sabbath is so important to God, is because *you're* important to God.

Finding Balance

Are you a work-a-holic?

I don't know about you, but it's not normal for me to take a day off. What is normal for me, however, is to go and go and go until I get sick. Then, I'm forced to rest... until I get better and the cycle continues.

Don't you think there has to be a better way, friends? If you're in this group with me—the group that never rests, never sabbaths, never takes a day off—then you probably think so, too!

But there's another group out there who needs a better way also: the group who only rests. You struggle to find motivation to do anything, and you lean toward the lazy side of life. Your way of life isn't pleasing to God, either.

See, this is where it gets tricky. Because some of us need a hug and some of us need a little push. Can't we just meet in the middle?

According to Exodus chapter 20, we were made for two things:

1. We were made to work.
2. We were made for rest.

Finding the balance between these two things is crucial when it comes to hearing from God. It's crucial to your ability to say yes to Him.

I had a mentor tell me years ago that he wanted all seven days of his week to be aimed toward eternity. I was intrigued, so I asked him to tell me more.

His week starts on Sunday morning. It's a priority for his family to be in the house of God, surrounded by the people of God, under the anointing of God. After church, they get lunch as a family, and after lunch, he does all the things he doesn't *love* to do, but has to do. He hangs the picture frame that his wife has been asking about for weeks. He mows the lawn. He takes the trash out. Then, he watches football at night, rests, and gets ready for the week to come.

Once the work week hits, he gives five days of hard, solid work to his boss. He works for his boss as unto the Lord as Colossians 3:23 says. Now, if you're keeping score at home, this guy labors hard for six days. He works for his boss, he goes to the soccer games, and he ensures the health of his wife's heart.

But come Saturday, he ceases. He Sabbaths. The phone gets turned off, the emails get shut down, his mind takes a breath, and he rests.

I've always looked up to this man because his Sabbath looks like a vacation every week for his family. And honestly, maybe that's the best way to put it. Sabbath can and should be like a family vacation once a week.

Now, let's get really practical here. **A Sabbath is anything that rejuvenates your soul and points you towards Christ.** Anything that makes you want to do the happy dance should be done on your Sabbath. For some of you, that's hiking. For some, it's camping. For some, it's mowing grass or gardening. For some, it's painting. Whatever it is that rejuvenates your soul, it should be enjoyed as often as possible, notably, on your Sabbath.

Find what rejuvenates you and take time to do it. Give yourself 24 glorious hours of rest every single week for the rest of your life. I mean come on, doesn't that sound amazing?

Pancakes and Bacon

I've just made a decision for my family. I refuse to fall into the American fallacy that I have to be busy all the time to be productive. In fact, as the spiritual leader of my home, I'm commanded to ensure that my family gets a weekly day of rest. I have made the decision that I am going to work hard and labor for six days, but come Saturday, we're going to party. We're going to live like it's a vacation.

So, hand me my sweatpants, whip up the pancakes, pull out the orange juice, bring out the bacon, (and not that turkey bacon! I'm talking about the thick, applewood, hickory smoked bacon!) and we're going to eat pancakes and bacon to the glory of God.

We're going to go on a road trip.

We're going to put the windows down and sing loud.

We're going to go hiking.

We're going to laugh so hard together we cry.

We're going to live life at least once a week like we're on vacation because God designed it this way. He designed us to work, but He also designed us for rest.

A glorious 24 hours to rejuvenate your soul and fix your attention toward heaven. This is Sabbath, and it's crucial for the Yes Generation. If we don't hear from God, we won't be effective for the Kingdom. So, take time friend. Let your soul take a deep breath. Eat pancakes and bacon. Laugh a little bit. Give yourself some space to Sabbath. Don't take yourself so seriously all the time.

I'll end this chapter with a verse of Scripture:

"Beloved, I pray that all may go well with you and that you may be in good health, as it goes well with your soul" (3 John 1:2).

In other words, I hope life is going well, kids are doing well, wife is great, life is good. I hope your job is paying you a reasonable wage and you're finding fulfillment. I hope your health is in good shape, and you're taking time to exercise and take care of yourself.

And then, just after the comma: *"...as it goes well with your soul."*

In other words, you can only be as good on the outside as you are on the inside. If your soul is not healthy, you will not be healthy. And if you are not healthy, your *yes* will not be healthy. You can say yes all you want to the things of God, but if your soul is tired, your yes will burn out.

The solution? Take time to Sabbath. Make it a part of your schedule. Find the rhythms of rest and watch God blow your socks off with how much more effective you will be.

LITTLE JIMMY, DODGEBALL, AND PRAYER

It's probably the most terrifying moment in the life of any grade school student: The moment during recess when people start picking teams for a game.

You remember this, don't you? Typically, the most popular kids in class would be named the "Captains," and then they would begin the process of picking their teams. Of course, the most athletic students would be picked first. And as name after name was called, running through everyone's mind was the thought, *"I don't want to be the last person picked"*.

Now, I know it's not a big deal in the grand scheme of life, but when you're in your pre-teen years, it's a big deal. Nobody wants to be that person!

I know some of us are a long way from middle school now, but just imagine this with me for a second. You're there as the captains are picking their teams. And you know what everyone else knows: *There is one person who you absolutely do not want on your team.*

Let's call him Little Jimmy.

At all costs, you must keep Little Jimmy off of your team. Because if Little Jimmy is on your team, all hope is lost. You might as well just pack up and leave.

Poor Little Jimmy, right? I hope you weren't the Little Jimmy of your middle school, and if you were, my deepest condolences.

What does Little Jimmy have to do with anything? Well, here's the confession of a Pastor, often times in my own life, I've treated prayer a lot like Little Jimmy.

I wouldn't say it like that, but my prayer life certainly revealed that. Far too often, I've made prayer my last resort—the last option to pick when it's the only one I'm left with.

Really and truly, prayer shouldn't be our *last resort*; it should always be our *first response.*

Jim Cymbala said something in his book, *Fresh Wind, Fresh Fire,* that absolutely shocked my prayer life.

He wrote: *"We are not New Testament believers if we do not have a prayer life."*

Wow! Honestly, he couldn't be more spot on. How can we confidently say we have a living, growing, active relationship with God if we don't have a strong prayer life?

I'll just go ahead and hit you with the hard truth God revealed to me: The reason we don't pray more is because we don't truly believe it works. Maybe you've tried to pray for days, or months, or maybe even years, but nothing is changing and certainly nothing is shifting. I have been there more times than I can count. I'm with you on this, and I hope this chapter challenges us in ways we've never been challenged. I hope this chapter stirs something on the inside of us that revitalizes our prayer lives.

"I'll be praying for you."

Have you ever said that? I know I have! Because of how often that phrase gets thrown around, I'm convinced that prayer is the most overpromised and under used resource for Christians all over the world. I would be so curious to know how many times we say things like, *"I'll pray for you,"* and then actually take the time to be quiet before the Lord, still our hearts, and focus our attention as we approach the throne boldly with the need we've promised to present to the Lord.

Or maybe we say things like, *"Well all we can do now is pray."*

Let's just kind of throw a Hail Mary since nothing else worked out. When things don't go the way we hoped, often we make prayer the last resort.

Oh Lord, help us on this!

If I read my Bible correctly, there are so many examples of the way prayer works in powerful ways for the believers.

Joshua prayed 13 words in chapter 10. It wasn't long, and it wasn't extravagant, but it was focused. He prayed 13 words that were full of faith, and what happened? The sun stood still for 24 hours.

In Acts chapter 16, it says, *"About midnight, Paul and Silas were praying and singing to God, and suddenly, there was a great earthquake"* (Acts 16:25-26). That earthquake caused the very foundation of the prison walls to start shaking.

In Psalm 3, David prayed that God would be a shield around him. He asked that there would be an army of tens of thousands of God's angels around him on every side.

Elijah prayed that fire would come down from heaven and burn up all the lies of the false gods.

So, what's the takeaway? Prayer is not a last resort. Prayer is not a Hail Mary. Prayer is a sun-stopping, prison-shaking, earth-quaking, lie-consuming fire that comes down from heaven as a weapon given by God to His children. But let's let the elephant walk back into the book, most of us could use a spark to our prayer lives.

Contrary to what the world might tell you, prayer is not weak. It's not feeble, and it certainly hasn't been debilitated. I believe God is calling His church into an audacious prayer life like the heroes of our faith experienced.

He's asking us to give up on praying small, feeble, little, wimpy prayers and to step into praying big, audacious, powerful prayers that are full of faith. So big that when they come into existence, there's no way you can take credit for it. I believe God is waking up the sleeping giant known as the Church, and it's going to happen when God's people believe for more in their prayer life.

So, before we go any further, answer this question: How are you doing with your prayer life? If, you're anything like me, sometimes it feels like Little Jimmy—a last resort or a Hail Mary of sorts. If that's you—let's encourage one another into a deeper relationship with the Lord through prayer.

Prayer provides posture

Prayer provides posture. More specifically, prayer provides God's posture, which in turn, changes our posture.

In Revelation 4, John wrote: *"I immediately was in the Spirit; and behold, a throne was standing in heaven, and I saw One sitting on the throne"* (Revelation 4:2).

In Revelation 20, he said, *"Then I saw a great white throne and I saw Him who sat upon it"*(Revelation 20:11).

And finally, Isaiah 66: *"Thus says the Lord, 'Heaven is my throne and the earth is my footstool'"* (Isaiah 66:1).

Are you seeing a pattern? It's abundantly clear in Scripture that first and foremost, there is a throne. And on that throne, there is One seated. And the best news you'll hear all day today is that it ain't you.

Whew! We can all collectively take a deep breath. We're not on the throne, the world doesn't revolve around us, and it doesn't rest on our shoulders.

Take a deep breath

Did you notice something about the One who is on the throne? Of course, we found out that it's not you, but look again.

"I saw a great white throne, and I saw Him who sat upon it."

Prayer provides posture. What's God's posture? He's seated upon the throne. Why does that matter? I'll tell you why I think it matters. I rarely ever see someone who is stressed out, and worried, and anxious *sitting*. Typically, if someone is anxious, or nervous, or worried, they have a pace to them. They walk back and forth in the room. Are you a nervous person? I am. When I'm nervous, I bite my nails, I pace back and forth, and I play with my beard. The last thing I want to do is sit down!

But notice God's posture: He's sitting down on His throne. That should be such a breath of fresh air to us. Our God is seated on the throne. He is not worried, and He is not freaking out. He is not looking down at the world we live in thinking, "Oh me, I didn't see that coming. What should I do? Should I cause another flood? No, I promised I wouldn't. Should I bring another plague? That won't work. What should I do?"

God is not pacing the golden streets of glory worried about what's happening on Earth. He knows exactly what's happening down here! He created it all. Everything is either ordained by God or filtered through His hand. Either way, He is still in control.

I want you to see a God today whom Psalm 113 says this about: *"The Lord is exalted over all the nations, His glory above the Heavens. Who is like our God, the One who sits enthroned on high!"* (Psalm 113:4-5).

Psalm 19 says this: *"The heavens declare the glory of God, and the sky above proclaims the work of His hands"* (Psalm 19:1).

Psalm 145 says, *"Great is the Lord and greatly to be praised; His greatness is unsearchable"* (Psalm 145:3).

I can promise you one thing today, friend. God is not in heaven worried about what we're seeing here on Earth. It may look bad to us, but it's not catching God by surprise. There is a peace that passes all understanding that dwells on the inside of you by the indwelling of the Holy Spirit. We can say with Paul, "I am perplexed, but not crushed," because our God is enthroned upon the praises of His people, enthroned to the highest place, and He is *seated* on His throne. We can declare with confidence that we know what's happening in our world, we're not in denial, but we're also not worried. We are aware but not anxious. We're informed but not impaired.

Our God is still on the throne. So, take a deep breath, because He is not freaking out.

Do not be anxious for anything

Really Paul? Anything? Don't be anxious about anything?!

Seriously? Out of everything Paul could have said in Philippians 4, he went with, *"Do not be anxious about anything"* (Philippians 4:6).

Let me ask you a sobering question: How are you doing with that one? Because if I can be honest, I will be the first to say that I have failed at this tremendously.

It's almost as if Paul doubles down here in the next verse: *"But in everything, by prayer..."* (Philippians 4:6).

Paul said do not *be* anxious. That word "be" means "to exist in or occupy for extending periods of time." In other words, do not *exist* in the things that cause anxiety. Notice Paul didn't say that we shouldn't *feel* anxious. He said not to *be* anxious. There's a big difference in feeling a sense of anxiety and being gripped in a perpetual state of anxiety.

Anxiety can be paralyzing; it can be crippling. It's normal to feel anxiety. It's called being human. We live in a broken world. You may disagree with Paul on this, and that's okay, but he seems to be saying the answer to the incessant anxiety or fear in our lives, is by *prayer.*

Got chains?

Prayer is a form of worship, and worship is a weapon—a mighty one at that. Anxiety will drive you to focus on the mountain, but prayer drives you to focus on the mover of the mountains. Worry will drive you to stay awake at night pacing the hallway, but prayer forces you to stop, quiet yourself, and focus on the One who reigns above it all.

So, if you've got some chains holding onto you in life right now, I've got good news for you: I know the One who's a chain breaker. If you need some freedom, I know the One who shatters every shackle and crushes every chain. You need a way where there is no way? I know the One who's a way maker!

You know Him, too! And prayer is the avenue to get to Him.

Prayer reminds us that there is One who sits in the heavens and scoffs at His enemies. Prayer reminds us that the earth we're living in right now is an ottoman for His feet. And because the Master is seated, you can take a deep breath. When the Master stands up, you know things are about to start unfolding. Until then, trust in God. Take a deep breath and remind yourself who is seated on the throne.

Do you know the reason that God is still seated? It's because *the work is finished.* There's nothing more to accomplish until the return of Christ. The victory has already been claimed. God is still reigning, and He is still ruling.

I refuse to be a captive to anxiety. I refuse to be a slave to worry and fear. Instead, I want to be free. I think you probably do, too!

If we want to be people of victory, we better have a substantial prayer life. Martin Luther is famous for penning, "To be a Christian without prayer is no more possible to be alive without breathing."

Charles Spurgeon once said, "True prayer is neither a mere mental exercise nor a vocal performance. It is far deeper than that—it is a spiritual transaction with the Creator of Heaven and Earth."

If we want to be people who are believing God will move greatly on our behalf, we better have a vigorous prayer life. If we want to see life change for the students on our campuses, the leaders of our businesses, and the people in our spheres of influence, we better have a vibrant, expectant prayer life.

Prayer is how we live in the fullness of God. Prayer is how we live in the abundance of God. It's literally the means by which He has given us to communicate with Him.

Dismantling the schemes

Did you know the enemy of your soul is actually scheming against you? Scheming to steal, kill, and destroy all the plans that God has over your life?

Let me give you something to consider. If somebody wrongs me unintentionally, I can usually move on pretty quickly. But when I find out that somebody pre-meditated an attack against me or my family, that just takes it to a whole other level!

Listen friends, the enemy of your soul is premeditating attacks on your life. Ephesians 6:11 says we must do this: *"Put on the whole armor of God, that you may be able to stand against the schemes of the devil."*

A scheme is pre-meditated. A scheme is thought of in advance. The devil is scheming against us. And if I was the enemy of your soul, you know what I would do? I would try to devalue and dismantle the greatest weapons that you have against me. I think that's the strategy in any battle. Dismantle the weapons that are most deadly against your opponent.

So, can I suggest something to you? Is it possible the devil believes in prayer more than you do? Is it possible that the devil knows how powerful the prayer life of a believer is against the schemes he is planning?

Is it possible that if we saw everything happening in the spiritual realm and how effective our prayers were, that we would ever cease to stop praying as Paul said in 1 Thessalonians 5:17?

What I am trying to call us into is a prayer life outside of Sunday morning. If the only time we're spending any kind of time in prayer is on Sunday morning, or before a meal, then we're never going to make it against the schemes of the enemy. If the only time we're spending on our knees going to war for our families, and our schools, and our nation is on a Sunday morning, then we're going to be in trouble.

The enemy has devalued the weapon of prayer in our eyes. And sadly, I believe many of us have fallen for this trap. We think of prayer as a nice and noble gesture, but we don't see it as the weapon that God intended for it to be in our lives.

Let me try and paint a picture for you that was helpful for me.

If I was your enemy, I would try and keep you so busy

during your day that you'd never have time for prayer. On the way home from a busy day at work, I would get you to "wind down" by listening to the radio, music, podcasts, or anything to keep your mind distracted and your heart unsettled. When you got home, I would make your home life so busy that there would be no room or margin for any kind of prayer time. When the time came for you to get into bed and have a little bit of quiet time, I would try and ensure that your mind would still be running and your heart would still be unsettled because of all the stuff going on in your life. The purpose? To leave no room for quiet and solitude that might give you an opportunity to hear from God.

See your enemy knows that if you develop a prayer life, he stands no chance. If you begin speaking out the promises of God over your life, he has no shot. If you begin going to war for your family, you can begin to cover your family in prayer. In those areas where he's clearly trying to get you to stumble, if you are calling out the promises of God over the lies that he's sending your way, he doesn't stand a chance. The enemy simply can't stand against the believer who has a strong, and developed prayer life.

Sadly, I think many of us who call ourselves Jesus followers are so busy and so occupied that we have given up on our prayer life. Or at the very least, we've treated prayer like Little Jimmy on the playground. It has become the last resort. It's become the Hail Mary when we need a miracle or a 25 second blurb before we start eating food. We may not say it like that, but I think it's probably true for a lot of us.

Here's where the rubber met the road for me. It was about a year ago where I took an inventory of the last seven days of my life. How much of it was spent in prayer? How much of it was spent before the Father seeking His face? I had to come to the awkward, embarrassing conclusion; it wasn't much time at all. Maybe this is true for you too?

Didn't God say this through the writer of the Chronicles?

"If my people who are called by my name humble themselves, and pray, and seek my face and turn from their wicked ways, then I will hear from heaven and will forgive their sin and heal their land" (2 Chronicles 7:14).

The Yes Generation is a chosen people who are not giving up on their prayer life. This is a generation of people who are not giving up on seeking God through prayer.

I'm not talking about praying before your meal or once before you go to bed (although both of those are great!). I'm talking about a prayer life that kicks the devil in the teeth and steps on his throat while he is down. A never ceasing kind of prayer life like the Apostle Paul had. A never fading, never ending, constant line of communication between you and your Heavenly Father.

A prayer life is essential for the Yes Generation because prayer is how we live in abundance with our God.

Talk about a dangerous yes. A Christian with a developed and vibrant prayer life is incredibly dangerous against the schemes of the enemy.

We need to make the decision to not neglect prayer. Corrie

Ten Boom once said, *"When a Christian stops praying, the devil shouts for joy."*

Charles Spurgeon is notable for his quote saying, *"If God be near a church, it must pray. And if he be not there, one of the first tokens of his absence will be a slothfulness in prayer."*

Jim Cymbala wrote in *Fresh Wind, Fresh Fire, "It is a shame so many churches no longer seek or appreciate this spiritual gifting from God. A heart that prays and a church that gives itself to communion with the Lord — these are two of the great secrets that bring God's blessing in untold ways upon the earth. "*

If we saw the ripple effect of our prayers, we would never cease to pray. All spiritual power is linked to praying in the Spirit. If our churches are not praying, isn't that a loss? Even if the auditoriums are full to capacity, if no one is seeking God in prayer, isn't that a loss?

The devil isn't terrified at all by a big church, he is terrified by a praying Church. He knows that when we link our limited resources to God's unlimited power, the kingdom of darkness will be damaged.

May the enemy shake in terror when he realizes the Yes Generation is waking up to the power of prayer.

NO ONE ELSE IS COMING

No one else is coming.

Five words, but wow, are they packed with power and emotion! There's something spine chilling about those words, isn't there?

No one else is coming.

They seem so final. So lifeless.

Imagine this scene:

An American soldier is in enemy territory about to be taken by enemy forces. He is bunkered down, crying out on the radio for help. Bullets are ringing through the night sky as airplanes fly above. Smoke and dirt are everywhere as the heavy fog of war fills the sky.

"Please send help! I'm going to die out here!" cries the soldier.

Moments go by that feel like hours as the soldier continues

to cry out for help.

Imagine the filmmakers of this movie flash back and forth to scenes of the soldier's family. Here, the soldier comes to realize that if somebody doesn't come quickly, he will never see his wife and little girl again. If somebody doesn't come quickly, he will leave behind a family who loves him and needs him.

The silence of the radio is deafening.

Finally, a glimmer of hope. On the other side, a distant voice comes through all the static.

Time stops. Everyone is on the edge of their seat. The voice answers back.

Soldier....

The radio static goes in and out...

No one else is coming.

Five words. So dull. So bleak. So final.

No one else is coming. I'm sorry.

I think about this phrase a lot. It has radically shocked my spirit, especially when I think about the people in our spheres of influence who do not know Christ. That simple phrase has lit a flame inside of me that cannot be extinguished. I hope it does for you as well.

There is a world around us crying out for help. A world looking for someone to throw them a rope from the spiritual battle they're fighting. And if someone doesn't come quickly, they will spend an eternity separated from God.

The reality we live in, is that there is an eternity waiting for every single person who is walking the Earth right now. I know it's not something most of us feel comfortable talking about, but part of that eternity is a place of destruction called hell—a place awaiting those who do not know Christ.

But the good news of the Gospel is that there is also a place of eternal satisfaction and beauty awaiting those who are found in Christ. A place called Heaven that God designed for every one of His sons and daughters to live in perfect harmony and joy with Himself.

Long before we ever walked this Earth, God initiated a plan of reconciliation for the world—a plan that allows those of us who believe in Him to spend eternity with Him. And believe it or not, *you* play a major role in that plan.

Yes, you!

Even with your flaws and blemishes, God wants to use you. He doesn't need to. He doesn't have to. But still, He *chooses* to.

And let me remind you, *no one else is coming*.

No one else is coming to your workplace to share the gospel.

No one else is coming to your gym to share the gospel.

No one else is coming to your business to share the gospel.

No one else is coming to your college campus to share the gospel.

The mantle has been given to *you*, as an ambassador for Christ to share the gospel.

God's plan from the beginning was to reach the world using people like you and me.

Could it be that God has strategically placed you, a Christian with the Holy Spirit living inside of you, where you're at right now to share the message of Jesus with people in your sphere of influence?

You are God's plan. And there is no plan B.

Not me!

I know what a lot of you are thinking right now:

God can't use somebody like me.

Well, with all due respect I'm here to tell you that you're mistaken.

There is a point in the book of Romans that many would consider the hinge point of the entire Bible. It's found in Romans 1:16. There, Paul writes, *"For I am not ashamed of the gospel."*

That word "not" is a double negative in the original language. The Greek word is *"ou me."* It would be better translated as, "I am no, not ashamed of the gospel". It doesn't make sense in our language, but readers in the first century would have just taken a gasp.

This is an emphatic no. This is without a doubt, no never.

Let me show you another time when this same Greek word shows up.

In the first chapter of Joshua, God tells Joshua in verse 5, "*I will never leave you nor forsake you.*"

The word *never* is the word "*ou me.*"

I will never, no never, leave you nor forsake you.

It's a double negative, and it doesn't make sense in our language, but in the original, it's so very powerful. God is telling Joshua that there will never, no never, be a circumstance or situation where He will ever leave him. He knows things will get tough and begin to look bleak, but when they do, Joshua can just remember this promise: *I will never, no never leave you nor forsake you.*

That's exactly the same sentiment—the same no never—that Paul is using in his verse. He is never, no never, going to be ashamed of the Gospel. If persecution, trials, or pain come his way, he will never, no never, be ashamed of the Gospel.

So, here's where Paul would suggest we need to start: If we want to be effective for the Kingdom and make a real echo in eternity, we cannot under any circumstances be ashamed of the Gospel.

And so, the obvious question now is: Are we? Are we

ashamed of the Gospel?

Because I know what the church answer is, *"Of course not! Not me! Never! Ou me!"*

But I also know in my own life (and maybe you can find some common ground with me here) that there have been many times where I knew God told me to go and talk with someone or pray with someone, and yet, I shrunk back in the face of all the *"what if's"* and I was afraid.

What if I'm rejected?

What if I don't have all the right words to say?

What if I look like an idiot?

What if…?

And what I think most of us want to believe is that we're just not equipped to do this, but I think the hard truth is this: In that moment, I am ashamed of the Gospel.

Maybe you've never been ashamed of the Gospel, that's wonderful. And when you finish this chapter you can go ride away on your magic carpet. But for the rest of us, there are many times where we shrink back.

But here's some really good news. The hope of any community is always found in the believers of that community.

Let me say that again so you don't read over it. *The hope of any community is always found in the believers of that community.*

It's not found in any government system.

It's not found in any school system.

It's not found in any workplace.

As wonderful as all of those things are, the hope of any community is found in the believers that make up that community. The people who make up the government systems, and school systems, and workplaces.

The point is this: if believers rise up with a "never, no never" mentality, then every sphere of influence they're in can have hope. That means your favorite coffee shop, your home, your neighborhood, and yes, even your workplace can be full of hope. But to see this happen, it's going to take the believers to rise up like never before and say yes to the things of God.

Wrong expectations

To be honest, I think the reason I spent so much time not coming alive in the things of God is because, for so long, I had the wrong expectations of God. For the longest time, I lived my life like God was going to open up the clouds, stick His finger down into the Earth, and start moving things around with His hand.

Now, of course I didn't think He would *literally* stick His finger down into the Earth, but I sure was living my life like He would. That was my skewed expectation. Even my prayers showed it. I would see someone in need or distress, and I would pray, *"Lord, please send them exactly what they need. Send someone to help them exactly the way they need it."*

But it wasn't until recently that God revealed something new—something different—to my heart.

I have sent what they need. I have sent someone to help them. It's you.

Wait, what? Me?

Ou me.

We expect for God to move in the Earth and send the greatest revival this world has ever seen, but typically, we separate ourselves from the equation. Yet when I look all through the pages of Scripture, the Bible shows a thread that rages completely against how many of us expect God to move.

Throughout the Scriptures, anytime God wanted to accomplish something on Earth, He chose to raise up a person to help Him do it.

Now let me clarify. I am not at all saying that God is handcuffed by our faith or lack of faith. He is sovereign even over our inability to act. But when God chose to do something in the earth, He chose to raise up a person to help Him do it.

For example, when He saw the wickedness of the world and sent the flood so all of humanity would be saved, did Jesus come down and physically build an ark Himself? No, He raised up Noah to do it.

When He chose to build a nation, did He send a bunch of

storks to fly over the nation and deliver all the children? Of course not! He raised up Sarah and Abraham.

When He wanted to deliver His people from the tyranny of Pharaoh, what did He do? He hardened Pharaoh's heart and raised up Moses. Why didn't He just do it Himself? Why couldn't He split the Red Sea from heaven? He totally could have, but He chose to use an incredibly flawed man named Moses and had him lift up the staff towards the water. He *chose to use a person.*

When Goliath stood and mocked the one true King, did God shoot His heavenly slingshot to take him down? Nope! He raised up David.

When God wanted His house built, He raised up Soloman.

When God wanted to do a new thing in the Earth and needed to get His message across, He raised up Isaiah.

When God wanted to rebuild the temple, He raised up Haggai.

When God wanted to take the promised land, He raised up Joshua.

Are you seeing the trend here? Anytime God wanted to accomplish something in the Earth, He *chose sovereignly* to raise up a leader. Not because He was handcuffed, but because He sovereignly chose to set up a co-operation, even with the most broken of people. Why does God continue to use broken people? Maybe He is trying to communicate a message to us. He doesn't need *perfect* people; He simply needs *available* people.

Religion tries to tell you that God can't use us because we're broken. But when I read my Bible, it becomes apparent that our brokenness can actually qualify us the most to do what God is calling us to do. Because it's in our brokenness that He gets the most glory.

Isn't that great news?

He designed it this way.

Genesis 1:26 seems to suggest that maybe God designed it this way. It reads, *"Let us create man in our image and let them have dominion over the fish of the sea and the birds and the livestock, and over all the earth."*

Do you see it?

*Let **them** have dominion.*

From the very beginning, God created a system where He would be King, and we would be His ambassadors. He would be sovereign and in control, yet *we* would have dominion in the Earth to accomplish His plans.

He would be the King; we would be the ambassadors.

This is what 2 Corinthians 5:20 speaks about when it says, *"Therefore we are ambassadors for Christ, God making His appeal through us."*

Notice something important: *God making His appeal, through us and in spite of us.*

We are famous for praying, "God, come and move in the Earth." But I wonder if we would slow down a little bit and listen for God's voice, His response would be, "I already did. And I've handed the baton to *you.* "

We're praying for God to move, but God is beckoning us to move. Yet how much of my life is spent not moving? How much of our lives are spent just sitting around waiting?

Here's the part that absolutely wrecks my heart: *No one else is coming.*

This is a mantle that God has given to you and me. If somebody in China does not here the Gospel, we have to take responsibility for it. If somebody across the street does not hear about the finished work of Christ, that falls on you and me.

This completely messes up our, *"Let's just throw up a prayer and hope something happens, "* kind of theology. This completely ruins the thought process that says, *"Let's just throw up a prayer, but not really change anything about our lives. Sure, I'm hoping for a move of God! But for now, I'm just going to watch Netflix"* kind of theology.

If we want to be a part of the Yes Generation, we desperately need to believe that no one else is coming, and our mindset has to shift. Our prayers have to shift. Our expectations have to shift. We have a responsibility, the ability to respond.

To think that God has actually given us this responsibility is exciting and terrifying all at the same time!

The time is now

I'll end the chapter with possibly the most bizarre story in all of Scripture to me. The story unfolds in Exodus chapter 8. God sent Moses to go talk to Pharaoh, who was the King of Egypt. God told Moses to tell Pharaoh the now-famous line: *"Let my people go,"*

But the threat came with some stipulations. In this specific section of Scripture, God warned Pharaoh that He would send a plague upon the country if Pharaoh didn't let His people go. The plague you might be wondering?

Frogs.

Yup, frogs.

God said there would be frogs coming out of every crevice you could ever imagine. Out of their homes, their beds, their ovens, everywhere their eyes could see, there would be frogs.

Pharaoh didn't believe Him, and so, long story short, the frogs came, exactly as God said they would do.

In a panic, Pharaoh finally comes to his senses and calls Moses. He basically says, "Hey Moses, give your God a call and plead with Him that I will let the people go if you take away all these frogs."

Pay attention to that word: *plead.*

When you plead with someone, you're desperate. When you plead with someone, you're on your last option. At this point, Pharaoh is exhausted. He just wants this issue fixed.

And sure enough, Moses asks God to remove the frogs, and guess what God's response is?

"Certainly. Set the time. When do you want the frogs out of here, away from your servants and people and out of your houses?" (Exodus 8:9)

What? This is great! The plan is working! Pharaoh will be so excited! No more frogs! Woo hoo!

So, Moses goes to tell Pharaoh the great news, and Pharaoh now has the opportunity to remove all these blasted frogs from the country. All he has to do is say the word. Just say when, and God will remove the frogs.

And yet do you know what Pharoah's response is?

"Tomorrow" (Exodus 8:10).

Wait, what? *Tomorrow?* What do you mean *tomorrow?* You've got to be kidding me! Why in the world would Pharaoh wait until tomorrow?

The disease of tomorrow

In the context of frogs, it seems bizarre, right? But honestly, I have to ask myself this very same question. In light of eternity, isn't it bizarre that the people of God aren't active in their faith today?

Why in the world do I keep putting off the Kingdom plans of God until tomorrow?

Something I've found about my own life is that I put a lot off until tomorrow. Some call it procrastination, I call it the *disease of tomorrow.*

Tomorrow I will hang the picture frame.

Tomorrow I will mow the lawn.

Tomorrow I will get serious about the things of God.

Tomorrow I will put God first in my life.

Tomorrow.

It's a disease. And before we know it, ten years have gone by, and yet when we look back over our lives, we have no eternal stock.

In the meantime, yes, we've been to church, but we haven't *been the church.* Yes, we've prayed before our meals, but we've never truly sought-after God with our whole heart. Yes, we've checked a few things off the list, and we've reached some goals, but have any of them been God goals?

Let's be the kind of people that make the decision that *today* is the day we will live for God.

So often we're waiting until tomorrow. But *today is the day the Lord has made.*

Because after all, *no one else is coming.*

We're not even guaranteed tomorrow. James tells us in chapter 4 verse 14 that our lives are *"but just a vapor".*

The time is now.

The day is today.

The moment is the one right in front of us.

I believe it's time for the church to get her zeal back. I believe it's time for the church to get her passion and focus back. There are so many things that people get excited about in our culture, and I believe it's time for that passion and excitement to cross over into our faith.

"I am not ashamed of the gospel."

It's time to get that same kind of extreme authority that Paul had. The kind that only comes from being filled by the Spirit of God Himself.

The reality is, life is short, and eternity is really, really long. Don't you want your life to amount for something in eternity? Let's make today count friends.

No one else is coming.

The torch is ours. The baton has already been given to us, and there is another generation coming right behind us.

A SUSTAINABLE YES

It's early in the morning and the fog has just started rolling over the North Georgia mountains.

I think to myself, *Ahh, nothing like an early fall morning in the mountains.*

The truck is warm and I'm in no hurry what-so-ever. Perfect start to the day.

I notice my gas light is still on.

I think to myself, *It's been on for like a day and a half. I'm not even sure if I'll make it to the gas station at this point. I'll take it easy and surely, I will make it.*

There's really two people in this world. Those who fill their tanks to the brim when you get down to about half of a tank, and those who wait until the light comes on, pushes it a few more days, and then only fill their tank halfway back up. I'm unashamedly the latter.

Have you ever been driving to get somewhere, and you start thinking about something completely random that needs to get done? And to your surprise, a few minutes later you end up driving to the totally wrong place? This happens to me more than I'd like to admit.

I was headed to the gas station until I finally came to myself when someone started knocking on my window.

What the?...

"How may I serve you today sir?"

Where in the world am I?

I look up only to realize I drove straight past the gas station and I was in the drive-through of Chick-fil-a.

I thought to myself, *do I explain how I got here? Or do I just order a chicken biscuit and move on?*

"Uhm..."

A few seconds go by and I respond, "I'll just take a chicken biscuit."

Ugh! Distraction!

Every time it happens, I get more frustrated than I probably should.

I like to be efficient and I like to be very systematic. It really bugs me when something isn't being done effectively. I took an Enneagram test recently, and I scored off the charts as a 1. Apparently, this effective and systematic approach to life is a side effect of being a 1. In short, we like things done quickly and perfectly. And that's why I get so frustrated when I have to do things twice, or go the long way, or take a route that isn't efficient, all because I wasn't paying attention!

Here's my point.

There was a time in the book of Exodus when Moses was getting ready to lead the Israelites out of slavery. The Pharaoh at that time was a pretty terrible leader, and the Israelites had been enslaved for 430 years. God had given Pharaoh plenty of opportunities to let His people go free. In fact, God sent ten plagues just to try and get Pharaoh's attention.

But God raised up Moses to lead the charge and finally lead the Israelites out. So, they begin the process of walking toward their freedom.

Shortly after, there's a bizarre scene in Exodus 13 where God sends pillars of clouds and fire to guide the Israelites to their freedom. They had to be thinking, *Wooo! This is great! How exciting! We're just a few moments away from being set free after 430 years of this mess! Our ancestors' ancestors have been praying for this day, and we get to be a part of it!*

Pretty exciting stuff, right?

They head out, following the clouds by day and the fire by night. But then, something even more bizarre happens. God doesn't lead them by the land of the Philistines (Exodus 13:17), which would have been far quicker. Instead, He leads them by the way of the wilderness.

I want to use this principle of "going the long way" as our illustration for gaining a sustainable yes in our lives. If you haven't noticed, we have an enemy who is trying to attack us on every side and destroy us. So, having a sustainable yes, in the midst of a dangerous yes, is important to the Yes Generation.

Now, we have the benefit of knowing the end of this story—God miraculously splits the Red Sea so the people can walk through on dry ground with walls of water on both sides. It's an inspiring, empowering, and exciting story, one that we know ultimately ends well. But you've got to remember, Moses didn't know the end of this story. He was living this story out in real time. And in real time, he had to trust and follow God's leading. He needed a sustainable yes, even when it didn't make sense.

So, even though it would've been shorter to go through the land of the Philistines, Moses had to tell the people they couldn't go that way. Even though there were fewer obstacles the other way, they needed to go the way God was leading them. Even though it would be more efficient to go by the land of the Philistines, Moses had to tell the people they needed to go toward the Red Sea.

Just for the record, this would have driven somebody like me nuts.

I imagine the Israelites must have been thinking to themselves, *Wait. You want us to go that way? Toward the Red Sea? This is a suicide mission! Pharaoh's armies are huge! They will kill us, Moses! We don't stand a chance! You're going to sacrifice the entire nation of Israel with this one bad decision!*

They must have thought Moses had lost his mind! But Moses knew that God said go toward the Red Sea, and so, that's what he had them do.

I think this is where so many of us struggle the most in our faith. When God tells us to do something that our minds can't make sense of, we struggle to understand and say yes to His leading. Have you ever had a moment where your heart desires to have faith, but your mind can't make sense of it? It's like your mind and heart are constantly in the middle of a boxing match, raging against each other in the ring.

Our minds always intend on making sense of a situation. And when things don't make sense, well, our minds freak out.

Trials to training

The world of social media doesn't help this trigger, by the way. Social media has rewired our brains to see our lives through the filter of everyone else's perfect, wonderful, amazing lives. We expect our lives to look like the equivalent of or better than what we see on social media platforms. Rather than living the beautiful lives that God has planned for us, we watch everyone else live the ones they present on Instagram.

It's a pretty sick cycle if you think about it. The people

we're watching are simultaneously watching other people live their lives, too. So, in reality, no one is really living their lives; we're all just watching everyone else live the version of their lives they post, and we live trying to keep up with everyone else's highlight reels.

It's a pretty sick cycle, actually.

I say all that to say that when our lives don't appear "Instagram worthy," our minds try and make sense of it. When we don't get the "Insta" miracle, or the "Insta" breakthrough we want, our minds struggle to make sense of it. The problem lies in the fact that our minds can't fathom the reality that God would ever take us down a route that's longer, less stable, and full of obstacles.

Let me say that another way to expound. Anytime we have to go the 'long way' or the 'hard way' we automatically assume it's the devil. But in Moses' case, it was actually God Himself who took them the long way. Our minds want the shortest, quickest, and easiest route possible, and when we get the exact opposite, we can't seem to make sense of it.

But I think there's a better way. I think we need to all understand this: We need to understand that what looks like *trouble* is often the *training* that God uses to produce in us the muscle memory we need to make a sustainable *yes*.

What good is it if we have an entire generation of Jesus followers saying yes to God, but then, after a little bit of pressing and a whole lot of trials, we find ourselves walking away from the very thing God called us to? What good is it to have a bunch of people who say yes to the things of God, only to give up on Him as soon as things don't make sense?

Not good at all!

In fact, it would be counterproductive. In fact, it would be the worst thing possible because it shows the world around us that God's plans for our lives aren't in fact good; it gives the impression that the plans of God are meant to take us down a path of destruction.

But let me stop here to encourage you with this: *That couldn't be any further from the truth.*

Wisdom or Revelation

We can't fathom in our small, finite minds that God would ever lead us down a path that isn't the easiest route. Our knee-jerk reaction when we find ourselves in a season of pressing, or obstacles, or trials is to automatically believe, *this must be an attack of the enemy.* But is it possible that what you think is an attack of the enemy might actually be a blessing from God? Is it possible that what you're trying to pray away could be what God is using to create in you the muscle memory needed for a sustainable yes? Is it possible that some of the things you're trying to find an easy way out of in your life could be the very things you'll be praising Him for in five months? I believe if we learn to trust God to handle the process, the promise can come forth.

God didn't send the Israelites on the route that was easiest or shortest; He took them directly into the wilderness. That seems odd, doesn't it? Well, this isn't the only time something like this happened in Scripture! Take a look at Matthew 4 with me.

Here, Jesus is baptized in the Jordan River. It's a beautiful moment in history where the Godhead is shown perfectly on display. We've got Jesus the Son being baptized, the Holy Spirit descending on Him like a dove, and the Father speaking over His Son, *"This is my beloved Son, with whom I am well pleased"* (Matthew 3:17).

But then, the very next verse says this:

"Then Jesus was led up by the Spirit into the wilderness to be tempted by the devil" (Matthew 4:1).

Did you catch that? Jesus was led *intentionally* by the Spirit into the wilderness. Doesn't this seem strange? That the Father would intentionally lead the Israelites into the wilderness and then turn around some 1,500 years later to intentionally lead His Son directly into the wilderness? If we can be honest for a second, I think it's safe to say this isn't a view of God that many of us like to talk about. But I think it's an important view to take on in order to have a sustainable yes. God can do the impossible, but He often calls us to do the impractical in order to get there.

A friend of mine shared something with me while we were at CrossFit that has shaped so much in my faith. He said, *"revelation and wisdom are two totally different things."*

Read that one more time and try and wrap your heart

around it. Revelation and wisdom are two totally different things.

Wisdom might have told Joshua to get out his sledgehammer and start banging on those walls. But revelation said to put the sledgehammer away, walk around these walls seven times, and blow a silly trumpet until you take the city.

That's not wise at all. In fact, it's impractical, but it was revelation.

Wisdom might have told Gideon to build a massive army to take the city, but revelation told him to cut the army down to 300 people to fight an army of more than 100,000.

Wisdom might have said to go straight through the land of the Philistines, but revelation told Moses to go toward the Red Sea instead.

Wisdom tells us to do everything we can to make life simple and convenient. Revelation says to take up our cross and follow Jesus.

See the difference? One makes total sense, and the other sounds ridiculous! But we must remember when we're in a season of life that seems peculiar and insignificant that wisdom might tell us to throw the towel in, this is too much, but revelation teaches us to stick it out and stand firm. After 6 laps around the city walls, Joshua probably felt pretty silly, but it was when he stuck it out, stood firm, and took another lap that the miracle came forth. It was in the 7th lap that he showed that his yes was a sustainable one.

The fight for your eyes

These days, everything is fighting for your eyes. Marketing experts suggest that most Americans are exposed to 8,000 ads per day. That's a lot of fighting for your mind, eyes, and attention! In fact, I recently read that social media companies are trying to get children using social media outlets like Facebook, Instagram, and Snapchat as early as possible so they will be addicted to it for the rest of their lives. The earlier they win them, the more money they will make over time.

Horrible, right?

Well, it's a struggle for all of us. It doesn't matter what age, demographic, or ethnicity you're a part of, everybody is fighting for your attention.

Let me ask an obvious question: Do you think the devil isn't aware of this? Do you think he's just sitting by hoping we accidentally fall into sin? No! Of course not! This is why we see all the time in Scripture it is beckoning us with power and authority to fix our eyes on Jesus. God knows that the devil is fighting hard for our attention every single day!

You need to fight for your eyes, friend. It's not easy to stop scrolling and comparing your life to everyone else's. It's not easy to stop watching porn. It's not easy to put down your screens. And because it isn't easy, we need the endurance to see it through. To have a sustainable yes.

Hebrews 10:35-36 says this:

"Therefore, do not cast away your confidence, which has a great reward. For you have need of endurance, so that after you have done the will of God, you may receive the promise."

We all want the promise, but we despise the process. We all want the resurrection but refuse to go through the cross. But the writer of Hebrews says that if we will endure through the process, the promise will be received with fullness of joy.

Hebrews 12 talks about running our race with *endurance.* That's the key word: endurance. Anybody can run, but to say yes to the things of God and make a real kingdom impact in the earth, it takes endurance. It takes a sustainable yes. According to the writer of Hebrews, there is a connection between our eyes and our endurance. The writer goes on to say:

"Looking to Jesus, the founder and perfecter of our faith" (Hebrews 12:2).

What's interesting is that in three verses, the writer uses the word *endurance* 3 times. That word in the Greek means" to bear up under with patience." Strong's Dictionary defines it as, "the ability to withstand great pain or hardship, to endure and bear bravely." If I could put it into my own words, I would say this: Endurance is the ability to carry on even in the face of fatigue, pressure, and unfavorable conditions.

Now that's a really interesting concept, because most of us don't want to bear up under *anything.* If there is any pain attached to it at all, it's the plan of the devil. If it takes us through extreme hardship, then we are out of the will of God. We don't want to wait for anything, and we certainly don't want to endure anything. In fact, I feel like that word *endure* is a Christian cuss word nobody wants to talk about. Why is that? Well probably because we live in the age of technology where we can download something in 3.5 seconds, and everything is right at our fingertips. We live in a microwave generation.

Forget 10-day shipping! We can get it in 7 days with this new company called Amazon. Once 7 days takes too long, we can have it in two days with Amazon Prime. When two days takes too long, we have Amazon Now, so we can have it two hours! We have apps like SeatGeek and OpenTable so we can have tickets to a show or reservations to a restaurant within seconds. If you can't find a ride, no worries! Just order an Uber to pick you up in three minutes. Uber wasn't even a word a decade ago, now it's a 3.1 billion dollar company.

Believe it or not, there was a time where we actually had to go to Blockbuster to get a movie we wanted to watch. Does anybody remember Blockbuster? It was basically the days of the devil, because it meant we had to get out of our pajamas, put on appropriate clothes, get into our cars, drive all the way to the video store, pick out the movie, get back in the car, and drive all the way home. Now, we can get any movie at any time instantly. We don't even have to wait for it to download anymore; you can start watching immediately!

Look, I'm not saying there's anything wrong with any of this. I'm the most impatient person you'll ever meet, so I actually love this age of immediacy. I'm just saying it's changed the way we live; it's challenged our ability to endure.

I'm sure we'd all love to be able to download an app for endurance, but there's no easy way to get there. Most of us want to be delivered *from* everything, but I believe often times God wants to take you *through* it so He can develop in you the muscle memory needed for the great things He has planned for you. But if we don't see it through the right lens, we'll begin praying away the very thing God is trying to use to build our muscles of faith needed for endurance.

My concern is that we're raising up entire generations of people who won't know what endurance is if we tripped over it. Millennials, Baby Boomers, and generation Z the same. We're medicating ourselves out of endurance. We're pulling ourselves out of the ability to withstand anything. We're missing the chance to build character through endurance. We all want instant ease and instant promotion, but as soon as it requires a bit of pressing, we assume it's not the will of God, and we walk away from the very thing He may be trying to develop in us.

What I'm trying to say is that maybe we need to toughen up a bit. This letter to the Hebrews was written in a time of tremendous persecution. In this time, it wasn't easy to be a Christian. People were losing their jobs, friends, and many of them even their lives. And if I could sum up the whole letter in one word, it would have to be *endurance.*

We live in a similar world today. People in America are being marginalized for what they believe. People across the globe are being persecuted and killed for their faith in Jesus. It's not easy to raise your children to be sexually pure in a sexually flooded world. It's not easy to be morally pure in a culture that's anything but. It's not easy to endure. In fact, I can promise you that it's a whole lot easier to just give up, or at the very least, not continue to stand firm.

But I'm here to call up a generation and encourage you in this: We must stand firm. We must endure. We must continue on as soldiers in the army of the living God. We must.

Luckily, the writer of Hebrews gives us the solution. He says, *"fix your eyes on Jesus"* (Hebrews 12:2). In other words, see how He operated, and follow accordingly.

Jesus operated on a daily basis with the help of the Spirit literally since the first day He was in Mary's womb.

In Luke 1:35, when the angel appeared to Mary, the angel declared, *"The Holy Spirit will come upon you, and the power of the Most High will overshadow you."*

Luke 1:41, *"When Elizabeth heard Mary's greeting, the baby leaped in her womb and Elizabeth was filled with the Holy Spirit."*

Luke 3:16, *"John answered them all, 'I baptize you with water. But one who is more powerful than I will come, the straps of whose sandals I am not worthy to untie. He will baptize you with the Holy Spirit and fire."*

In Jesus' inauguration into ministry, Luke 4:1 says, *"Jesus, full of the Holy Spirit, left the Jordan and was led by the Spirit into the wilderness."*

Jesus operated out of the power of the Holy Spirit, and He intends for us to as well. Look at His plans for us...

John 14:26, *"But the Helper, the Holy Spirit, whom the Father will send in my name, he will teach you all things and bring to your remembrance all that I have said to you."*

John 16:13, *"When the Spirit of truth comes, he will guide you into all the truth, for he will not speak on his own authority, but whatever he hears he will speak, and he will declare to you the things that are to come."*

How did Jesus endure? By the power of the Holy Spirit.

How did Jesus have a sustainable yes? By the power of the Holy Spirit.

If we're not careful in both embracing this endurance in our lives and modeling it for the lives of others, we will end up raising up an entire generation of half-way Christians who drop out of the front lines of faith because people told them they could bypass the sanctification process. The goal is not to see how much we can do *for* God; the goal is to see how much we can *become* like Him. And the more we become *like* Him, the more we will accomplish *for* Him.

But that process isn't easy. And if we're going to be more *like* Jesus, we have to remember that a major part of His story was enduring through the cross. At the end of

Hebrews 12:2, the writer gives us such encouraging words. It writes, *"For the joy set before him he endured the cross, despising it's shame, and is seated at the right hand of the throne of God."*

There's that word endure again. If we're going to be like Jesus, there *will* be a cross to take up. I know that's not very popular or fun to talk about, but without this truth, we've been sold a bad bill of Christianity. When we get told, *"Everything will be beautiful and wonderful all the time, all you have to do is follow Jesus"* we're setting ourselves up for an unsustainable yes.

As challenging as this is, it's so important we grasp this. In fact, Jesus warned us of this. He said in John 16:33, *"I have said these things to you, that in me you may have peace. In the world, you will have tribulation. But take heart; I have overcome the world."*

The key is endurance.

When His followers misunderstood Him, Jesus endured. When the Pharisees lied about Him, Jesus endured. When His disciples decided to fall away from Him, Jesus endured. When Peter denied Him three times, Jesus endured. When the Sadducees tried to trap Him and make a mockery of Him, Jesus endured. When the disciples scattered, Jesus endured. When Judas betrayed Him for 30 pieces of silver, Jesus endured. When He pleaded with the Father in the Garden of Gethsemane, Jesus endured. When the temple guard arrested Him, Jesus endured. When the soldiers mocked Him and ridiculed Him, Jesus endured. When they put a crown of thorns in His head, Jesus endured. When they hammered Him to a cross, Jesus endured. When all the forces of hell came against Him, Jesus endured.

And the same Spirit that did all of that in Jesus, is living on the inside of you and me. Therefore, we *can* run our race with endurance!

My faith reminds me that God is for me. And even if the wind comes against me, or the world be against me, I can endure. Even if they nail my savior to a cross, I've got faith to believe that in three days, He's coming up out of that grave holding the keys to death, hell, and the grave. Therefore, we can endure in Jesus' name!

The position you're in right now is on purpose. It's a process. It's called sanctification, and it's crucial for the Yes Generation. Behind every calling is a crushing. Behind every crown is a cross. Don't get fooled by the "Instagram faith" that leads you to believe everything is supposed to look perfect and beautiful all the time. Some of the greatest men and women who serve the Lord in the most powerful ways don't do anything that would make it to the highlight reel of social media. They're just normal, everyday people stepping out and saying yes to the things of God. They're people who are willing to endure.

Wrap it up dude

This whole chapter started with the Israelites going the long way to the Red Sea. You know how this story ends, right? God purposefully brought them into the wilderness so that He could bring them to the Red Sea. There, He could split that bad boy in half and let them walk through on dry ground so Pharaoh's army could be drowned in the sea. It's one of the most remarkable miracles that God ever did in the history of Israel. But here's the crazy thing: God would later encourage the Israelites to forget about what He did there.

In Isaiah 43, God said: *"He who makes a way in the sea, a path in the mighty waters, who brings forth chariot and horse, army and warrior"* (Isaiah 43:16-17).

What's He talking about? You guessed it! The time when He split the Red Sea. Here's the interesting part. The very next verse God says, *"Remember not the former things, nor consider the things of old"* (Isaiah 43:18).

Why? Well, it goes on:

"Behold, I am doing a new thing; now it springs forth, do you not perceive it? I will make a way in the wilderness and rivers in the desert" (Isaiah 43:19).

The very thing that was an anchor in the history of Israel, God tells them to forget. Can I encourage you with something? I believe that God wants to do even greater things *now* than He did back in the days of Moses! Isn't that exciting to consider? That God wants to do now even greater things than He did thousands of years ago when Moses saw the Red Sea split, and Elijah saw fire come down from heaven, and Joshua saw the Jordan River split and the sun stand still. As amazing as those events were, they don't even hold a candle to the new thing that God is doing after the death and resurrection of Jesus Christ.

In order for us to get in on what God is doing in the earth, we need a lasting and sustainable yes. Not a wishy-washy, here one day and gone the next kind of yes. But we need a sustainable yes. James put it this way in chapter 5, verse 12: *"let your yes be yes, and your no be no."*

God is not looking for perfect people, He's looking for available people. I wish I had time to talk about how *not perfect* Moses was for the job. I wish I had time to talk about how *not perfect* Joshua, Abraham, David, Samson, Gideon, and on and on we could go! None of these people were *perfect*. But God is not looking for perfect people; He's looking for available people.

It's exciting to think that God actually desires to use someone like you and me.

So, will you say yes to the process of God? Will you run your race with endurance in the face of exhaustion, pressure, and unstable conditions?

Is it possible you're on the cusp of God splitting the Red Sea in your life? Bringing down the walls of Jericho on the 7th lap?

Don't lose faith because your mind is trying to make sense of it. Sometimes you have to walk through the wilderness and take another lap around the walls.

Let's be the generation who says yes to the process of endurance and sanctification to see God do something so beautiful in our lives.

SWEATPANTS AND ICE CREAM

One of the biggest challenges we face in our culture is focus. If you're anything like me, you're in the process of learning how to juggle nearly one million different things, all the while trying to do it all for the glory of God. But what if there was a better way? What if there was a more fruitful way to do this crazy journey called life?

A mentor once said something to me that I'm still working to get a better grasp on. He said, "The more you try and do, the less you will actually get finished." At the time he said it, I immediately thought to myself, *Well that just can't be true. I've got to be productive. To be successful, I've got to be alert and oriented times five.*

In his book, *The 4 Disciplines of Execution,* Sean Covey describes how we need to focus on "the wildly important." In other words, everything else needs to be cut out in comparison to what's *wildly important* in life. Doesn't that sound a lot like the heart behind this book? Pushing aside the things that are temporary in order to step into the things that are eternal and wildly important by saying yes to the right things.

Focus is crucial to the Yes Generation.

I always think of focus in regard to the sun. The sun is a 10,000-degree ball of fire at the center of the universe. At its core, temperatures can reach 27 million degrees Fahrenheit. That's really hot! But because the earth is such a perfect distance from the sun, the rays from the sun are too weak to start a fire on their own.

Maybe you'll remember this trick from your childhood, but if you take a magnifying glass and focus the sun's rays, you can light a piece of paper on fire in seconds. The principle is clear: On its own, the sun's rays aren't powerful enough, but when you focus the rays, you've got yourself a torch.

The same principle is true for the human experience, and it's crucial for the Yes Generation. Once all our energies are headed in the same direction and focused on one goal, we become an unstoppable force known as the Church. A force that Jesus declared, *"The gates of hell shall not prevail against it"* (Matthew 16:18 KJV*).*

But to become all that God has called us to be, focus is crucial.

To say yes, you must say no

If you're going to say yes to the things of God, you must say no to the lesser things of life. I'm not saying those other things aren't good things; they just may not be the 'God things' that you've been called to do.

As the Yes Generation, we have to learn how to effectively say no. Let me say that another way for the people in the back. *If we want to have an effective life lived out for the things that matter, we have to learn how to effectively say no to the things that are good but not wildly important.*

I'm sure you've had this thought before: *If only I had more time in the day.*

Well, the reality is, we all have time for the things we chose to have time for.

It doesn't matter what your everyday life looks like—we all get the same amount of time in a day. And every time you say yes to giving your time to something, you're saying no to something else.

Time is everything. Time management is key, and energy management is crucial if you're going to be effective for the Kingdom. I do not want to live a life that is so busy and full of things that are meaningless and temporary that I miss out on the things that are of eternal weight.

Time is money

Imagine I handed you a check for $1,440. Now I'm not sure what that much money looks like in your world, but for me, it would get me pretty jazzed. (Does anybody say jazzed anymore? I think we should bring that back.)

Now imagine every single morning when you wake up, I hand you another check for $1,440. Pretty amazing, right? For anybody keeping up at home, that's an annual salary of $525,600. Not too bad!

Now, there is one rule that comes with this money. Whatever money you don't spend in the day doesn't roll over to the next. If you only spend $500 one day, the other $940 goes away. I don't know about you, but I would be so careful with every single dollar I had. I would do everything in my power to make sure every dollar was spent well and with purpose. I wouldn't want any of it to go to waste.

Well, here's some bad news: I'm not giving you $1,440 per day.

But here's my point: There are 1,440 minutes in a day. Every time the clock strikes midnight, the reset begins. We have another 1,440 minutes to spend as we choose. Every day, day after day, month after month, year after year.

Let's not over spiritualize this: your life will amount to everything you say yes and no to.

Read that again. *Your life will amount to everything you say yes and no to.*

An effective life is just simply effective days strung together.

So, how will you spend your time? In the same way you budget your money, I recommend making a budget for your time. Or to take it one step further, have you ever thought about creating a budget for your energy? I've talked with so many people who feel like they can't find their purpose in life. If I had a dollar for every time I heard the phrase, *"I just don't know what God wants me to do with my life"*, I could retire early. We're all trying to find our purpose. We all want to be a part of something bigger. But so many of us get distracted by the seemingly meaningless events of life and miss out on the eternal things God is doing all around us. We need to get our focus back.

If we're going to say yes to the things that God has planned for our lives, we'll need to get a whole lot better at saying no. In fact, this is a skill I'm trying to get better at myself. I want to get to the place one day where I can say no without offering any explanation. I'm not there yet, but I'm working on it. I'm excited for the day when I hit spiritual maturity to just say no. Period. No excuses. No reasons. Just plain no. What a glorious day that will be!

Down time is not wasted time

Wait a minute, I thought this book was about saying yes? Now you want me to say no? Make up your mind, Mike!

Trust me, it all makes sense! Because how you use your no is just as essential as how you use your yes. Maybe you're like me, and you want to please everyone. For people like us, saying no can be a big challenge. In this season of my life, I only want to say yes to three major things. My first and biggest yes is always going to be about being a son of God. Now before you mentally agree with me and try to move to the next point, let's stop and break that down.

Being a son of God first means I have to put God first. I have to budget time into my schedule for two people: me and the Lord. That sounds real good and real spiritual, but the problem for a guy like me, is that I struggle with down time. I feel like down time is wasted time. I always need to be moving, creating, building, and growing. If I'm not, I feel like I'm wasting time.

This approach to life came to a head for me a few months before writing this chapter. I found myself absolutely *exhausted* and slowly slipping into a small form of depression. I'm not talking about just being tired. I'm talking about tired on top of tired. I was absolutely wrung out. I had nothing left to give. Looking back, I feel so bad for the people who went through that journey with me at our church because I just literally had nothing to give back or offer to anybody. I fell into the trap of working myself to death, comparing myself to everybody, and never giving my soul time to breathe.

It was in that season I learned that in order to pour out to others in the most effective way, I have to take time to fill myself back up. In other words, for my yes to be most effective, I need to get really good at saying no. I have to find time where I intentionally fill myself back up—where I put my time alone with the Lord first.

If you don't get anything else from this chapter, at least take this:

Down time is not wasted time.

You need it. I need it. And we'll all be better for taking it.

The hard truth

All of us will come to this realization one way or the other—the realization that we are running out of time. At the time of writing this book, I am at the ripe young age of

27 years old. If statistics are true, that means I'm more than 35% complete with my life on planet earth. That's kind of daunting to think about, isn't it? The average life span in America is 78 years old. I'm not sure where you fall on the spectrum, but if this is true, I'm almost two-fifths of the way through my life already.

Life will happen so fast, and this whole thing will be over before you know it. Life is really short, and eternity is really long. 78 years isn't even a drop in the bucket compared to eternity. If that's true, then why do we spend so much effort and resources investing in the time here on earth? We work ourselves to death for 65 years just to be able to "enjoy" 13 years of retirement. We spend our whole lives killing ourselves for only 13 years on the back end of this life, when we have an entire eternity ahead to look forward to!

Something I learned as a young man that I am so incredibly thankful for is that **death either takes you *to* your treasure or *away* from your treasure.** If you're storing up in heaven, then death will bring you closer to your treasure. If you're storing up on earth, then death will take you away from your treasure. Even in this, your yes determines everything, and your no is essential. Both determine where you ultimately store your treasure.

We are a ticking time bomb just waiting to explode, and life isn't moving any slower. The hard reality is that for some of us, it will take absolute exhaustion for this to really sink in. You will read over this chapter and it will go in and out of your heart with no real conviction. Sometimes we have to get to the darkest places in our lives before this reality can really sink in—before we can realize that we're distracted by things that aren't wildly important. It may be a divorce, health issues, or extreme anxiety, but sooner or later, something will happen in your life that forces you to slow down and re-evaluate. That forces you to fix your focus.

You know, Jesus had this tremendous ability to stay focused. We talk so often about the *love* of God, the *mercy* of God, the *grace* of God, but have you ever stopped to think about the *focus* of God? So many times in Scripture, people tried to distract Jesus. The Pharisees tried, His disciples tried, Satan tried, and even His own family tried. Yet Jesus was able to remain focused on the mission at hand.

I'm learning that being sustainable in any area of my life requires a tremendous amount of focus.

There's no room for distractions in the kingdom plans of God.

But maintaining my focus is a process. In certain areas I'm extremely focused, and in some, I still struggle tremendously.

To have a healthy, thriving marriage and a healthy family life, it takes focus. To have healthy friendships, you guessed it, you must have focus. And certainly to have an impact in the Kingdom of God, it takes focus. To have anything that is worth anything in this life or the next, it takes focus.

So, here's the question: **Have we lost our focus on what's wildly important because we have become distracted by things that are wildly insignificant?**

Trying to stay focused in a world of distraction is hard. Trying to stay pure in a world of distraction is challenging. Trying to parent your kids in a world of distraction is exhausting. We all feel this tension and stress in one way or another. When you want to spend time with your kids, but all you can think about is the meeting your boss called for Monday. When you want to spend time in the secret place with God, but there are phone calls that need to be returned, and emails that need to be written, and employees that need your help. When you're trying to live your life, but you find yourself distracted, watching everybody else live theirs on social media.

Let's face it. In one way or another, we're all distracted. We all feel pulled apart. We live in the tension where this person wants this, or that person needs that, or she expects something that we don't feel like we can offer, or he requires something we don't have the energy to give. We want to serve and be there for people, but we're pulled in a million directions.

We're being devoured by distraction.

I can't tell you how many times I've felt like I was running around trying to do a million things for the glory of God. While it may be well intentioned, that certainly doesn't sound like a very overcoming life. And it certainly doesn't sound like the life Jesus calls us to live.

Like I said, I don't think I'm the only one who feels this tension. In fact, I think if I could use one word to describe the American church, it would be **distracted**. The enemy loves this. He would love to keep you distracted. Since he knows he can't *defeat* you, his best bet is to *distract* you. The enemy comes to steal, kill, and destroy! We all know that, right?

The enemy is deceptive. I don't know about you, but I've never had the devil knock on my front door dressed in a red jumpsuit, holding a pitchfork, only to say, *"Hey! I'm here to ruin your life today! Is that okay? Care if I come in? Have some coffee? Maybe chat it up a bit?"*

He doesn't work like that! The way the enemy comes to steal, kill, and destroy the plans that God has for our lives is by way of *distraction*. It's his most valuable weapon. The distractions are killing us—killing our joy, killing our marriages, killing our families, killing our relationships, and most importantly, killing our focus.

Time to wake up

I want to call the church to a spiritual awakening. Because the chaos and distraction are creating a breeding ground for the devil. The devil works best when things are chaotic and busy. The devil is simply waiting for an opportunity to catch you sleeping or distracted by chaos so that he can wreck your family, your mind, your marriage, and ultimately, the very calling that God has put over your life. And if we don't wake up and see what's happening, he will wreck all of these things right under our noses, all while we're too busy to see it happening. As C.S Lewis put it in *The Screwtape Letters*, *"Just keep them busy Woodworm. Busy, busy, busy."*

Overdoing is one of the deadliest things for us, yet ironically, it's one that is so rewarded in our culture.

Let me say that again in another way so it sinks in. *Overdoing is one of the most over celebrated diseases in our culture.* It's bragged about and often exalted above all else.

But I'm here to take some pressure off of you, child of God. Stop doing more than you were designed for. You do not need to feel bad for needing down time. Down time is not wasted time. Write that on your mirror, write it on your heart, and remind yourself of it as often as possible.

Down time is not wasted time.

Sometimes you need to unplug from everything in life and go to the beach. Sometimes the most spiritual thing you can do is go home and take a nap. If you're anything like me, sometimes you just simply need permission to take a moment and disconnect. Consider this chapter your permission slip from heaven. Down time is not wasted time; it's time to recharge.

Sweatpants and ice cream

I'll never forget some wise words from a dear friend. I was 24 years old, running my own business, and can confidently admit, I had no idea what I was doing. I may have acted like I knew, but in reality, I was just winging it and praying it would work out. After about a year of that, I began to feel all the weight from the pressure to perform and to be a leader—a leader I didn't feel like I was. It was an accumulation of all the different things that came along with being an under-equipped, young leader, but I called my mentor and told him that I didn't think I could do it anymore. I was done, ready to throw in the towel and run in the opposite direction as fast as Wile E. Coyote. I'll never forget the words my friend spoke to me over the phone.

He told me to go to the grocery store, get a tub of ice cream, go home, throw some sweatpants on, and eat every bit of the ice cream.

I, of course, thought that was weird. I expected him to give me six steps to become a better leader, or four ways to improve productivity, or ten ways to be a better boss. You know, something practical that would help me in my situation of being an underdeveloped leader.

Maybe he would give me some inspirational speech like Herb Brooks gave to the US Hockey team in the 1980 Winter Olympics when they defeated the Soviet Union?

"You were born to be a hockey player—I mean, a business leader"

"You cannot be a common man, because common men go nowhere! You must be uncommon!"

I thought he was going to say something productive like that.

Instead, he made me promise that as soon as I got home, I would take a shower, get in my favorite sweatpants, watch a few episodes of my favorite show (*The Office*, of course), eat the entire bowl ice cream, and get a good night of sleep. His advice has stuck with me for years. He said confidently over the phone, "You know, as silly as this sounds, don't ever underestimate the power of a good bowl of ice cream, a pair of sweatpants, and a good night's sleep."

I don't know what it was about that magic vanilla ice cream with peanut butter cups and chocolate fudge, but I woke up the next morning feeling great. I'm not saying it always works like this, but this time, it really helped. That day, I woke up with fresh perspective knowing that God had called me to this. And if He called me to it, He has equipped me for it.

It was a simple lesson, but profound in nature. Don't do more than you were designed for. Don't take yourself so seriously. Life is way too short, and the plans that God is dreaming for your life are way too important to throw the towel in. As Paul told the Galatians, *"Don't grow weary in doing good, for at the proper time we will reap a harvest if we do not give up"(Galatians 6:9).*

If your hustle doesn't allow you time to spend with the Lord, then you're over-extended, my friend.

Slow down.

If your hustle doesn't allow you to spend quality time with your family and kids around the dinner table, then you're overextended.

Slow down.

If your hustle doesn't allow you to spend time doing the things you actually enjoy in life—the things that are wildly important— then you're overextended. If your hustle doesn't allow you to throw some pajamas on, grab a bowl of ice cream, and watch your favorite show, then you are overextended. It's time to say no to some things and retake the ground that God intended for you to take.

If we want an effective yes, we must get really good at saying no.

COMMUNITY

Let me paint a picture for you.

My wife and I were living in a two-bedroom apartment in our small little town of Blairsville, Georgia. I was 25, and Becca was 22. We had just celebrated our two-year anniversary and were now frantically trying to get everything in our home in order for company that was on the way over.

Have you ever been there? Just stuffing things into a closet hoping nobody opens the door to find an avalanche of mess falling at their feet.

We were prepping our apartment for the arrival of the first ever leadership team meeting for the church we were dreaming about. We were so nervous to host, that we started getting ready almost five hours before they ever showed up! Becca put ice in the cups so early that by the time our company got there, the ice had melted. Unfortunately for us, the ice maker in our refrigerator was broken, and at that stage in our lives, we couldn't afford to get a new one. Another confession of a Pastor, I totally just acted like we poured water in their cups before they got there. They totally bought it.

Fun side note: This is the same apartment where I pulled the handle off the microwave door, and because we couldn't afford to buy a new one, I just screwed the handle back into the door. This created a great adventure every time you got something out of the microwave because you either got stabbed by the screw sticking out (ultimately leading to a potential tetanus shot), or you got your food. Those were some good days!

It was in this apartment that Vertical Church was born. It was messy, yet magnificent. It was awkward, yet awesome. It was crammed, yet perfect in every way.

As we were sitting in a circle with seven other families dreaming about the things God was dreaming about, we had no idea the adventure we were about to embark on together. I remember the first line that came out of my mouth that night.

I said confidently, "I believe God is calling us to start a church like a home."

At the time, it didn't feel all that profound. It didn't feel sexy, or exciting, or catchy. In our world, *everything* is glamorized. Everything needs to be in lights. Everything needs to be fancy and shiny. But that phrase was anything but fancy at the time.

God was calling us to start a church that simply felt like

home. A place where the hurting, broken, marginalized, unloved, and unchurched people could come and find rest and peace for their soul.

There's just something about *home,* isn't there? It doesn't matter what's happening around you, the moment you walk into your home, the stress and concerns of life just seem to grow strangely dim. That's the kind of environment we were dreaming about creating in our church. A place that wasn't an institution or an organization. A place that was about *real* people with *real* pains and *real* hurts meeting with a *real* God. And that's exactly what God has done.

The sad reality is that if you were to ask any ten people on the street what they thought of when they heard the word "church", I'd be willing to bet you could give them a million opportunities to answer, and none of them would respond with the word *"home."*

That's because the word church doesn't have the best connotations in our day and age. The real meaning has gotten lost somewhere along the way. And that real meaning is, simply put, *community.*

From the moment the Church started in Acts 2, it was designed to be a community of connected people— connected to God and connected to one another. A community that laughed together, cried together, and even fought together.

In fact, I'd argue the difference between a church of today and the church of the 1st century is that the people who made up the church back then weren't just connected; they were *committed.*

Committed means loving each other and serving each other.

Committed means celebrating soccer practice and job promotions together.

Committed means laughing with each other and crying with each other.

Committed means praying for each other.

I'm not talking about that, "I'll pray for you and then not really do anything," stuff. I'm talking about really seeking the Lord and bringing our brothers and sisters before Him in prayer.

Time and time again in the New Testament, the Bible shows the Church to be a community of people who have been likened to a family—connected and committed.

Don't you want to be a part of a family? Of a community? The Church is a family. Sometimes it's a dysfunctional family, but it's a family, nonetheless.

I can't think of a more important time than now to have a church likened to a home. In a time where suicide and divorce rates are on the rise. Children are growing up fatherless more and more. Anxiety is crippling more people than ever. There's never been a more crucial time in my lifetime for the people of God to be in a healthy, thriving community.

It's what we need

It was Abraham Maslow in 1943 who developed the "pyramid of needs." In this pyramid, he said that all humans have basic psychological needs, like food, warmth, water, and rest. We also have basic security needs, like employment and a deep sense of safety. Those make sense, right? Easy to understand.

However, the third tier of needs has always been fascinating to me. There, Maslow determined we need a sense of *belonging*. We crave a sense of community. And I think he's right! WebMD recently wrote a blog post that shows loneliness has the same effect on our bodies as smoking 15 cigarettes a day. Isn't that crazy? Being without some form of community can cause the same amount of damage to us as consistently smoking cigarettes.

That's because community is what we desire. We *need* a sense of belonging.

If you don't get anything from this chapter, at least take this with you:

True confidence is a byproduct of truly belonging.

Let me try and say that another way. True confidence is not a byproduct of *achieving*; it's a byproduct of *belonging*.

And if you think about it, this approach is completely and totally backward from our current worldview. How often do we think things like….

If I could just earn this status, I'll have confidence.

If I could just earn more money, I'll have a better sense of belonging and safety.

If I could just do this one thing more consistently, I'll have more confidence.

We all know how that ends, don't we? Maybe we achieve the thing, or maybe we don't. Either way, the confidence we get from it (if any!) isn't lasting. And that's because true confidence doesn't come from achieving; true confidence comes from belonging.

So, here's the good news for you today: **If you've given your life to Christ, you *belong* to Christ.**

God knows your name. In fact, He has given you a new name. A new identity. A new life. New dreams and new desires. He has made all things new. You belong to Him, and in that belonging, you are free.

Isn't everyone looking for the "1-2-3, how do I get set free?" combination? If only it were that simple! Can I give you some insight here? Become alive in the love of God. Because perfect love casts out all fears. Perfect love will deliver you from all sorts of issues. A sense of truly belonging will root confidence down in your soul and deliver you from an orphan mentality. It will give you a true confidence in your sense of belonging in the kingdom of God.

You're not a cast away.

You're not second class.

You're not thrown out.

You're adopted!

You're chosen!

God picked you!

Can we let that settle on our soul for just a moment?

God picked you.

Wow!

Marvin and Daisy

Becca and I have a dog named Marvin.

I know it's not the manliest thing you'll ever hear me say, but there, I said it.

He is a little white and black Maltese. He's super cute, and I like to imagine him wearing an argyle sweater, smoking a pipe, and drinking a nice glass of scotch. Oh, and he's an accountant, too.

Along with Marvin, we have Daisy. Daisy was a rescue puppy, and she is my girl. I am a little biased, but I truly think she is the best dog to ever walk the planet.

Marvin on the other hand is a spawn of Satan. I'm kidding... mostly.

What's interesting is that both of our dogs were hand-picked. There were multiple dogs that we *could* have chosen and brought home with us, but we *picked* Marvin and Daisy. We *selected* Marvin and Daisy. There was a moment where we said, *I want you to be a part of this family. We're going to love you. We're going to care for you. I can't wait to welcome you into our home.*

And I think that's exactly how God sees you. He chose you. He picked you. He adopted you and welcomed you into His family. And here's the cool part: He was really excited about it.

Let me say that again: He was really excited about it. His hand wasn't forced, and He wasn't guilted into this. He chose you. He could not wait to welcome you into His community and into the family of God.

It's so easy to *project* confidence in this day and age. We've got all kinds of social media pages where we can *project* confidence in so many ways.

But to *possess* confidence is a totally different thing.

When we come into the family of God—when we truly believe that He hand-picked us to belong with Him—we find a deep sense of confidence that we can truly possess.

True confidence comes from truly belonging.

You belong to God. You are His, and He is yours.

Let that settle on your soul today. Don't zoom past this section, take a moment to reflect on that glorious truth.

God chose you and He was excited about it. He didn't feel forced and didn't need to be convinced of it. He handpicked you for good works, in advance.

Something I struggle with...

I want to share something that is tucked deep in my heart. It's something I don't share with many people, but I want to open up to you about it here.

There have been a lot of times in my life that I stand up on the platform to share God's Word with our church and sense this feeling: *I don't belong here.*

I know my mistakes.

I know my flaws.

I know my struggles.

I don't belong here.

They'll see right through me.

But then I found a word—a revelation—about belonging that changed something on the inside of me. It didn't change my relationship with God; it changed my *confidence* in my relationship with God.

It's found in Hebrews chapter 4:16. And it reads like this:

"Let us then approach God's throne of grace with... fear."

Wait, did I get that wrong?

"Let us then approach God's throne of grace with... insecurity."

That doesn't seem right.

"Let us then approach the throne of grace with _____."

We can fill in the blank for days. The point is so many of us approach the throne of God as if we don't belong. But the real Scripture says this:

*"Let us then approach God's throne of grace with **confidence**, so that we may receive mercy and find grace to help us in our time of need"* (Hebrews 4:16).

True confidence comes from truly belonging.

But that's not often how we approach Him. We don't approach God like we belong. We tip-toe around the throne of grace. We're timid about stepping into the presence of the Lord. But last time I checked; my Bible says I can boldly approach the throne of grace to find help in my time of need.

So don't miss this! Approaching the throne of God like you belong is not arrogant. Understanding that you truly belong is not cocky or crude. It's confidence that the price has been paid. The blood has been shed. The veil has been torn. And because of that blood shed on the cross of Christ, we have been given access to the throne of grace. In fact, not stepping into the presence of God with confidence nullifies the work of Christ on the cross, and Paul told us in Galatians 2:21, *"Do not nullify the grace of God, for if righteousness was through the law, then Christ died for no purpose."*

It's not because of anything we've done or how great our devotion is. It's simply because God *picked us. He chose us. He selected us as His sons and daughters.* We have been given the gift of the Holy Spirit so we can boldly enter into the grace of God's throne.

We have been granted a sense of belonging that no amount of money could ever give. Because of Jesus, we have been granted a sense of belonging that no mansion on a hill could ever give.

The message of Jesus isn't, *"Belong only when you become."*

The message of Jesus—the message of the Gospel—is that Jesus *became* for you what you could never *become* for yourself.

Here's how I know:

"For our sake he made him to be sin, who knew no sin, so that in him we might become the righteousness of God" (2 Corinthians 5:21).

"For you did not receive the spirit of slavery to fall back into fear, but you have received the Spirit of adoption as Sons, by whom we cry, 'Abba! Father!'" (Romans 8:15).

"It is he who made us, and we are his; we are his people, and the sheep of his pasture" (Psalm 100:3).

"You belong to God, my dear children" (1 John 4:4).

And that's just to name a few!

Jesus did for you what you could never do for yourself.

Romans 8:15 says that the Holy Spirit in me causes my

spirit to cry out, *I have a Father!*

And because of the sacrifice of Christ, we have been granted access to walk into the throne of God *boldly. Unashamedly. Free from fear and shame.*

I don't know much, but one thing I do know is that there is nothing that will change you more than the reality of knowing that you belong to your Heavenly Father. Nothing will change you more than knowing that you are His and He is yours.

For many of you, this may be hard to fathom because of what your earthly father said about you. For others of you, the world has labeled you all kinds of different things.

But our Heavenly Father says you are chosen.

Our Heavenly Father says you are not forsaken.

Your Daddy says that you are a princess.

Your Daddy says that you are loved.

If only we had a deeper understanding that we *belong,* I believe our lives would never be the same.

Martin Luther once said this, *"If we could just understand the first two words of the Lord's prayer, the rest of our life with Christ would fall into place."*

You know what the first two words are?

"Our Father".

You belong to God. He is yours and you are His. Louie

Giglio said it this way in his book, *Not Forsaken,* "God is not a *reflection* of your earthly father; He is the *perfection* of your earthly father."

True confidence does not come when you achieve a bunch of goals. True confidence does not come when you reach a certain income. If you allow confidence to come from people, it can be taken away by people. If you allow confidence to come from success, it can be taken away by failure. If you live for someone's compliments, you will die by their critique.

We need a deeper sense of belonging, a deeper sense of our Father. True confidence only comes when you understand that you belong to a family bigger than yourself. It's the family of God, and that's where we find the ultimate sense of belonging for which we were created.

That's where we find our community.

Find your crew

Humans always gather together in little groups. Think back to your high school days. All the football players stayed together. Everybody in the band formed a little tribe. All the really smart people that most of us are working for now found their own little crew. Even the people who were 'anti-establishment' and didn't want to form a community ended up forming their own little community, right?

I believe the reason for this is because we serve a communal God. Our God created us for community, and because of that, it's in our nature to seek out community.

God is inherently communal: three persons in one.

The Father is in community with the Son, who is in community with the Spirit. The Spirit is pointing people to Jesus, and Jesus is drawing people to the Father.

He said in John 14:9, *"Anyone who has seen me has seen the Father."*

Jesus said in Acts 1:5, *"For John baptized with water, but in a few days, you will be baptized with the Holy Spirit."*

It's this great dance, as CS Lewis calls it, of the Godhead, three in one, living in community with one another. It's no wonder we are drawn to community as human beings, because we were made in the image of a communal God (Genesis 1:27).

Therefore, it is crucial that we find our crew. Our gang. The people we associate with and do life with. *Because we thrive in community.*

Pastor Craig Groeschel once said, "Show me the top five dominate voices in your life, and I will show you your future."

Isn't that so true? Show me the people you sow your live into, and you can almost guarantee the life you will reap.

When we get with people who are focused on the same mission—people who love God and who love the house of God—we discover that we thrive in community.

Rumble Strips

Have you ever seen the rumble strips on the side of the highway? The point of the rumble strips is to warn you when you start to drift off the road. And they do a phenomenal job at it. In fact, according to the Delaware Department of Transportation, they reported that fatal head on collisions have decreased by 90% when rumble strips are installed. Rumble strips are considered the most cost-effective, safety precaution that has ever been implemented on the roadway system.

The goal of a rumble strip is to warn you that you haven't drifted off far enough to hit the guard rail yet, but if you keep going on this trajectory, you will undoubtedly hit it. The rumble strips are designed to keep you going in the right direction and eliminate drift.

Do you see where I'm going with this?

I can't think of a better way to keep your life headed in the right direction and eliminate the drift than by having a community of people around you who are holding you to a Biblical standard.

The people you do life with act as rumble strips.

This is so crucial, because typically, we don't notice when we drift. In your marriage, you won't notice you're drifting until it gets so bad, you're considering divorce. In your finances, you typically don't notice you're drifting until you need to force yourself to go on a budget or your finances will be upside down. In your health, you don't notice you're drifting until something hits you so hard you find yourself in a hospital room.

You don't notice you're drifting unless there are rumble strips in place. And community is the best way to put spiritual rumble strips in your life.

If you have people around you who make the word of God a priority, the house of God a priority, and the people of God a priority, guess what? You've got kingdom greatness around you. As I like to say, you'll become guilty by association.

You need community in your life. In fact, I would go so far as to say you need to prioritize your life around good, Godly community. If that means you can't take a job in another part of the country because you will not have good community, then don't take the job. If that means that you can't do certain things because you won't have the right community, then don't do it.

Community is that important in God's economy.

If you're in a place right now where you have good, Godly community around you, I would suggest you do everything you can to stay right there in that community. Change your lifestyle. Downsize the cars. Downsize the house. Do whatever it takes to ensure you have Godly community around you. Because you were not only created for community, you were created to thrive in community.

Think about it like this. You are one small group away from the greatest spiritual growth you've ever experienced in your life. Or, on the other side of the coin, you are one small group away from the greatest spiritual decline you've ever seen in your life.

The common denominator in both scenarios? Having the right community around you.

Wait, that doesn't make sense?

In Genesis 2:8, God said, *"It's not good for man to be alone."*

In Ecclesiastes 4:9, Solomon said *"Two are better than one, because they have a great return on their labor. If either of them fall down, they can pick each other back up. But pity falls on the one who has no one to help them up."*

I think about Proverbs 24:16, *"For though the righteous fall seven times, they rise again."*

You know the number 7 in Scripture means *completely.* So that verse could read, *"For though the righteous fall completely."*

Terribly. Miserably. Though you have completely fallen, you can get back up again. I wonder how many people stayed down longer than they were supposed to because they didn't have anybody there to pick them back up again?

Deuteronomy 32:30 says, *"One can put to flight 1,000, two can put to flight 10,000."*

Wait, that doesn't make sense? It seems as if two isn't just doubly better than one, but in Kingdom economics, two is ten times better than one.

That's community. And that's what we were created for.

If you want to be a person who says yes to the things of God, then get yourself around other people who have said yes to the things of God.

Of course, I'm not saying you put yourself in a camp and completely remove yourself from the world. We can never reach a world that we abandon. That's not the point.

The point is to encourage us all to reach the world with the Gospel, while understanding that we need 3 or 4 people in our lives who will hold us accountable as we do. We all need a crew. I don't care how much money you make, how big your houses are, or how many cars you drive.

We all need community.

If you want to be a person who says yes to the things of God, get yourself around other people who have said yes with you.

Let's get together and change the world.

Are you up for it?

A HIGHER YES

This journey we've been on in this book has been absolutely life changing for me. I hope it has stirred up your affections for Jesus and your intimacy with the Father through the power of the Holy Spirit in you as well.

The #1 takeaway for me on this journey has been how powerful one little word—three letters and one syllable—has been for me.

Yes.

Maybe even more importantly, I've discovered how powerful the two-letter word—the companion of *yes*—is as well.

No.

Yes and no.

What hinges on those two words for us is remarkable. Our whole lives, the impact we make, the sphere of influence we reach—they're are all hinging on the things we say *yes* and *no* to.

Saying *yes* to the right things can open up a world of spiritual blessings.

Saying *yes* to the wrong things can open up a world of pain and trials.

Saying *no* to the wrong things can create spiritual margin in your life to draw closer and closer to the Father by the power of the Holy Spirit.

Saying *no* to the right things can leave you in a world of regret.

Yes and *no* are such an intricate part of our lives, but how often we are flippant in the way we use them.

The danger we run into as Christians is that we can *way* over spiritualize this whole thing. So, let's keep it simple. The way your life is going to play out is primarily defined by the things you say yes to and the things you say no to.

That is either tremendously exciting or excruciatingly crippling. To think that the God of the universe has given you and I the free will to be able to say yes and no to things that come in and out of our lives!

New year, new me

I always chuckle a bit when I hear this phrase: *New year, new me.*

You've heard something like that before, right?

This year will be different! This is the year I'll get back into shape! This is the year I'll grow closer in my relationship with the Lord! This will be the year I'm going to get out of debt! It's a new year, and it's going to be a whole new me!

What I'm always tempted to say back to that is, *I love it! I'm all for it! Let's change some things up in our lives, I think that's wonderful...*

But this new year will not create a new you just because the calendar changes.

I know that sounds kind of harsh, so please forgive me. I'm still learning this whole filter thing. But just because the calendar changes doesn't mean that the stress and tensions of life will change with it.

I know from experience that life doesn't really care what month it is. A new year doesn't mean anything more than a date on the calendar. The truth is that nothing is going to change in this next season of life if we don't get more intentional about our *yes* and our *no*. This next season of our lives will be just as busy as the last one if we don't learn how to prioritize in order to create margin in our lives.

Your yes creates margin. Did you know that? The world is fighting for your *yes*. Every advertising company is fighting for your *yes*. Businesses survive and thrive off of the consumer's *yes*.

The world is fighting for your *yes*. But here's the good news:

So is God.

A higher yes

So if our *yes* is this crucial in defining the kind of lives that we live, then the goal of this chapter is to recognize that as Jesus followers and children of the King with the Holy Spirit dwelling inside of us ready to break out like a kernel in a popcorn bag, here's what you and I need to realize:

We have been called to a higher *yes*.

I know that sounds exciting, but God has really been challenging me in this area. Because when I look back over my life, I see how often my *yes* has been negotiated. Maybe you do, too?

Because of life experiences, people walking out on you, or people treating you wrong, your *yes* can quickly become a *maybe*.

What previously was a resounding, hot, blazing *yes*, has suddenly turned into more of a, *yes*…but only *if it's comfortable.*

Maybe you'd even be honest enough to say that what previously was a *yes* has actually become a *no*.

Let me clarify. It's not that you don't love God. It's just that your yes has been negotiated. Your priorities have gotten out of whack and the boundaries that you used to have no longer exist.

Instead of saying *yes* to the right thing, we find ourselves saying *yes* to **everything**.

Back to the beginning

When God showed me this word *yes*, my first thoughts went something like this:

My schedule is already totally crammed and booked. My life is busy enough, and I don't want to have to say yes to another thing. In fact, I need to be saying no to more and taking things off my plate, not saying yes and adding more to it.

Maybe you feel the same way? The thought of saying *yes* to another thing in this season of your life feels crippling. It feels nearly impossible. There's no way you can make it work. If that's you, I hear what you're saying.

Here's what God has been showing me recently. He doesn't want to add *another* thing to my already overloaded plate. What I believe God wants to do is completely remove everything from my already overflowing and over-crammed plates, only to add back things that are wildly important.

God is looking for an available life—a life that has margin and space to be able to say *yes* to the things of eternity. After all, how can we say *yes* to the things God is calling us to if we have no margin in our lives to do it?

Yes and no

With our *yes*, we actually establish a few things. With our *yes*, the priorities of life become clear, which is crucial if we want to make an impact in eternity. And in our *yes*, we actually begin to establish boundaries for our *no*.

This is the most freeing, fulfilling revelation that God has given to me in a long time. **When you define your *yes*, you establish boundaries for your *no*.**

I don't want to live the rest of my life like a chicken with its head cut off. I don't want to be running through life doing a million things to the glory of God. I want a defined *yes*. I want a focused *yes*—one fixated on the things that matter. I want a higher yes.

I hope you do, too! If so, you'll need to define your *yes* to establish boundaries for your *no*.

Isn't that the way James put it in chapter 5?

"But *above all*" (James 5:12).

Let's just stop there for a second.

Above all.

In other words, of everything James teaches us about in his letter, he says this is the pinnacle. This is the most important thing you need to know. He saved the best for last.

"But above all…let your "yes" be yes and your "no" be no, so that you may not fall under condemnation" (James 5:12).

James is pretty clear. When you commit to something, commit to it. Don't let your *yes* be *yes*, until something better comes up and turns it into a *no*. Rather, let your *yes* be *yes*, and your *no* be *no*.

Let your *yes* be defined and clear in your life. Because if it isn't, you risk falling under condemnation

We do it to ourselves

Have we become a self-fulfilling prophecy? The things we're stressed out about, worried about, and extremely tired about are the very things that we have inevitably said *yes* to?

The enemy of your joy is not the people you work with or the job you find yourself in. The enemy of your joy is not your financial situation. The enemy of your joy is your inability to define and prioritize the yes in your life. Our entire lives are built off of the things we say *yes* to and the things we say *no* to.

There is no reason under heaven why you can't be a part of the *Yes Generation*. Even though it is dangerous, there is no reason under heaven why you can't shine more brightly than you have ever shined before in your entire life.

God has the capacity to do the greatest thing that He has ever done in your life. This is why it's crucial that we end this book with a resounding, powerful, and clear declaration that came out of the mouth of Isaiah.

It's found in chapter 26, verse 8. Two words, but packed with power:

"Yes, Lord."

There it is!

Yes, Lord!

And then here's the confession:

"Your name and your renown are the desires of our hearts."

I mean, come on! If we could get that verse tucked into our hearts as a burning inferno of passion, I'm telling you, the world will begin to change.

"Yes, Lord. Your name and your renown are the desires of our hearts."

Not my name.

Not my fame.

Not the name of the company I work for or the places I buy products from.

This is not me building my own kingdom, but rather, this is me acknowledging, your name and your renown are the sole desire of my heart and my life.

If we can aim our arrows at that bullseye, everywhere we set our feet and put our hands to can begin to change.

Warning!

So much of our conversations, resolutions, and desires are all about one thing: ourselves.

So many times, I have to check my heart and recognize that

what I'm pursuing is my desire, my passion, my dream, and it was all aimed at building my own little kingdom. So many of my conversations are about *finding myself.*

But the message of the Bible is not to *find yourself.* The message of the Bible is to *deny yourself.*

I hope you're with me on this, but I refuse to let my life come and go without making a Kingdom impact in the Earth because all I did was focus on myself. This is why we must say *yes* to the right things, not everything. This is why I'm convinced you should be a part of a generation of people rising up to make a dangerous yes. This is why I'm convinced you should join the Yes Generation.

Because right now, on the other side of eternity, there is a great cloud of witnesses who have run their races with perseverance. They are cheering us on as we run ours. I can promise you that they are not on that side of heaven going, *"Gosh, I really wish I spent more time building my own kingdom. You know, now that I'm literally in the throne room of God, it's not it's all cracked up to be. I really wish I had focused more on myself."*

No, they are on that side of eternity cheering us on! Encouraging us to go all in and give everything we have to make sure every *yes,* and every *no* is all aimed at something that actually matters in eternity.

It's time to get off the fence and say *yes* to God at a deeper level. We get one life, and it will soon pass. James 4:14 says, *"Life is but just a vapor."*

It is visible for a short time, and then it vanishes into thin air. We must make it count. Only what is done for Jesus and the building of His Kingdom on Earth as it is in Heaven will last.

The time is now

So, here we go.

Now is the beginning of a life lived towards eternity. Not tomorrow or someday soon. The time is now.

Will you go to the nations? *Yes.*

Will you go to your neighbor? *Yes.*

Will you remain when life gets tough? *Yes.*

Will you continue to love God when life gets stressful? *Yes.*

Will you put God first in this season of your life? *Yes.*

Will you join *The Yes Generation?*

Will you be unleashed for the kingdom plans of God in your life?

Let's do this, Church. Let's change the world, one person at a time.

One *yes* at a time.

God's greatest desire is that He wants your full on, resounding, blazing, passionate *yes.*

Join the Yes Generation.

It's a dangerous yes, but there is no other life.

ABOUT THE AUTHOR

Michael Medori is the Lead Pastor at Vertical Church in Blairsville, Georgia. Michael and his wife Rebecca are expecting their first child right after this book releases.

Michael and Rebecca both have a passion to see the Church of Jesus Christ come alive and make real kingdom impacts in the earth. Their passion is to see churches in small towns radically flipped upside down for the glory of God, equipping and engaging them to make disciples.